Slices

Tales of Bizarro and Absurdist Horror

By Scott Cole

Also by Scott Cole

SuperGhost

For you. Yes, you.

"The Regenerates", "Playtime", and "Cat Tree Summer" originally appeared in the *3 Stories* chapbook.

"Violins For Sale" originally appeared in *The Magazine of Bizarro Fiction,* Issue 11.

"Hole" originally appeared, in slightly different form, at *Bizarro Central.*

"Drive" originally appeared at *Bizarro Central.*

"Horns Up" and "The Pet" originally appeared in the *2 More Stories* chapbook.

"Brother Barry" originally appeared, in slightly different form, in *Rotting Tales.*

"Dates" originally appeared at *Weirdyear*.

"Scheduled Meal Service" and "Multi-Crabs" originally appeared in the *3 Bites* chapbook and the *3 Little Bites* chapbook, both of which quickly disappeared from the world.

"Rough Night" originally appeared at *Smashed Cat Magazine.*

"The Eater" originally appeared, in different form, in the *3 Bites* chapbook.

"666 Baby Jesuses, Give or Take" originally appeared, in slightly different form, in *Surreal Grotesque,* Issue 12.

Contents

The Regenerates

Sitting alone in this empty room, I become so bored that I decide to tear out my tongue and throw it against the wall. The fleshy mass smacks the eggshell paint job and sticks there for a second before falling limply to the gray carpet below.

The tongue just lays there, like a tired seal, for a moment, then suddenly begins to pulsate. Surprised, I pick myself up off the floor, and watch as the tongue starts to expand. It quickly grows a new mouth around itself—teeth, lips and all. A nose begins to form above it, while a chin appears beneath. The chin grows a neck, and the nose gives birth to cheekbones, eye sockets, eyes. Soon I'm staring at another me, fully grown and smiling back. I smile too, baring my now-bloody teeth to the clone. The other me tears its tongue out and throws it at the wall. Once again it sticks, falls, and begins to expand.

The minutes pass. There are a dozen of us here. Then fifty. It's a good thing the room has no furniture. Otherwise we would never fit. Soon, two hundred of us are standing shoulder-to-shoulder, pressed against each other. The walls must be straining to contain us all.

Suddenly the door bursts from its hinges, exploding outward, away from us. We all turn to look, surprised by the sound, and see the door lying on the ground. A moment later it starts to quiver, then begins to grow a new frame around itself. Soon there are eggshell-colored walls and gray carpeting—another complete room.

Half of us move in, and the tongues begin to hit the walls again.

Violins for Sale

"Violins for sale!"

Jonas was already awake, dressed in a bathrobe, making his morning coffee, when he heard the call from down the street.

The neighborhood had always been quiet. So quiet, in fact, that Jonas often wondered if anyone else truly lived on his street. He had never met any neighbors in the three months he'd lived there. He had never encountered a single soul, actually, had never seen a single person, had never heard a single voice, or evidence of anyone, ever. So the sound of a salesman, to say the least, was a bit of a surprise on a Tuesday morning.

Jonas padded across the room, to the window at the front of the house, not wanting to draw attention, despite the fact that he was insulated by some rather thick walls, and about a block of outdoor space.

"Violins for sale!" came the shout again. The voice boomed down the block, vibrating off the facades of the other houses. It was a solid, firm voice, with a rather sophisticated British accent.

Jonas peeked through the vinyl blinds that covered the front window, without touching them—just looking through the cracks—again, not wanting to draw attention. But he spotted no one outside. The voice was growing louder with each successive announcement, but the caller must have still been a half block away at this point. Then, suddenly, Jonas spotted him, several houses down.

The salesman was a very tall man, at least six-and-a-half feet tall, and fully dressed in a formal black pinstripe suit, despite the fact that the city was in the midst of a heat wave. It was a tuxedo, Jonas assumed, but something of an unfamiliar style, at least in his limited formalwear experience. The man wore a bowler hat as well, and had a thick mustache that curled upon itself at both ends.

"Violins for sale!" he shouted again, as Jonas moved from the window to the front door, hoping to get a better look. When he spotted the salesman through the peephole, he must have made a sound, as the man with the accent immediately turned toward his home, and began heading right up the front steps.

He rang the bell. Jonas froze in place, terrified at the thought that he might have inadvertently summoned the salesman, or that he might be able to see him through the tiny peephole. But he knew that was ridiculous. Peepholes were generally one-way things.

"Good morning, sir!" the man called out. "Interest you in some violins?"

Jonas shuddered. Could he actually be seen, somehow? He felt his heart thumping in his chest, and tried to steady his breathing. No, of course not. He would just need to remain still for another minute, and then surely the salesman would move on.

"You realize I can see you, don't you, sir?" he said. "You're wearing red and white striped socks."

Jonas looked down, and realized his toes were sticking out through the two-and-a-half-inch gap between the bottom of the door and the floor. He suddenly remembered he needed to buy mousetraps.

Jonas bit his lower lip as he undid the locks and opened the door for the overdressed stranger. The hinges squealed.

"Sorry, sir, but I don't play," he said, not even bothering with a standard greeting.

"Play?" the salesman retorted, cocking his head to one side. His eyebrows twitched as if they weren't attached to his face.

"Right," Jonas answered. "Violin. *Or any other instrument, for that matter.* I was never very musical, actually. Sorry."

"Wh—Ohhh, I see," the salesman said with a pursed-lip chuckle. "No, no—it's not *violins* I'm selling. It's *violence.*" His eyebrows twitched again, as he enunciated the final word to the best of his ability.

"Excuse me?"

"Yes, violence. I've got violence for sale."

"You've got...violence. For sale." Jonas shifted his feet, and placed a hand on the door frame, a subconscious act that served to block the salesman from entering. He was confused, and concerned.

"That's what I said, sir."

"I'm afraid I don't understand."

"There's not much to understand, sir. I peddle acts of violence. It's how I make my living."

"I see."

"That's right, sir. I can supply just about anything you're looking for, and at very reasonable cost."

"And how's that working out for you?" Jonas wasn't sure whether or not to believe the man, but continued to engage him regardless. He was curious.

"Oh, quite well! My trade is a rather popular one." The man removed a white cotton glove from his right hand, before extending it to Jonas. "Dr. Damage at your service!"

Jonas shook the man's hand, noticing the dark red flecks on his fingertips, the nails caked with what he assumed (provided the man was telling the truth) to be blood.

"You're a doctor, then?"

"Yes! Well...no. Just a fan of alliteration. So, what do you say? Can we make a deal of some sort? As I've said, my prices are quite fair."

"No. Thank you."

"You're certain? But I haven't yet given any specifics." Dr. Damage's eyebrows twitched again. They seemed unreal, as if they weren't actually there, but instead projected on his forehead, like film of two caterpillars, but with occasional missing frames.

"No, I'm good."

"Oh, I'm sure you are! And that's exactly what could make this even more interesting. Your skill, your powers of evasion...it could make for a bit of a challenge. You'd certainly get your money's worth, and I'd probably have a bit more fun than usual."

Jonas was intrigued, but still uncertain about whether the stranger on his doorstep was telling the truth, or was simply a madman.

"Look, we can start out small. How about a slap across the face?"

Jonas didn't respond.

"Or, or...stomp your toes? Poke in the eye? *Punch to the neck?* No? Alright then. I'll cut you. Chef's knife across the stomach. No? How about a broken nose? Broken arm? *Choke you?*"

Again, Jonas didn't respond. He just stared at the salesman. Dr. Damage took this to mean that he was unimpressed by his offerings. And so, he decided to step things up.

"Okay, okay. I can see you're a man of taste. No garden variety violence for you, sir, am I right? No problem. As I've said, I can offer virtually anything you can imagine. And if *you* can't imagine it, perhaps *I* can.

"I could kick your knees in. And I don't mean just break them. I would strike them at just the right angle, so that your legs would bend the opposite direction of how they do now. Be happy to do that for you, sir.

"Or... Nothing like a good flaying. Can't disagree with me on that one, can you, sir? I'd start at your toes, work my way up. Want patches of flesh left behind, perhaps some sort of design? Stars? Spirals? Butterflies? None of these poses any significant problem for me.

"Hmm. Skinning not your thing, then, sir? I could punch you in the bollocks for an hour. Burn your bum with a hot tea kettle. Cut the webbings between your fingers and toes.

"Just looking over your shoulder there, I can see you've got a bit of a mouse problem. That's quite a lot of droppings for one corner. Tell you what. Let's say I pluck out one of your eyes, collect a bunch of those pesky mice, and build a little diorama. Mice playing beach volleyball. What do you say? I'll even provide the sand. Make you a hell of an offer on that, and you'll have a keepsake too!"

Jonas continued to let the man talk. He had already said no a few times, and didn't foresee changing his mind.

"Of course, the thing about violence is, I don't have to do it to you. Have someone else in mind? Any enemies, sir? A high school teacher who failed you? An employer who never recognized your true potential? Someone who cut you off in traffic? A waiter who never refilled your water glass? How about one of these neighbors of yours? I've noticed people aren't particularly friendly around here.

"Of course, willing participants are welcome too, but I'll leave all that up to you.

"I could blow something up. Indeed, explosions are a specialty of mine! And I'm perfectly willing to travel, if that's what the job requires. Want me to tie someone up and burn their house down while they're still inside? Shall I book a helicopter ride for someone, then fire rockets at the aircraft? Got someone you're particularly upset with? I've designed a grenade that looks like a rectal thermometer. *Hmmm?*"

Jonas yawned. He hadn't yet taken a sip of his coffee, which was still sitting in the pot in the kitchen. He glanced back in that direction.

"Have a sick pet that you don't want to watch wither away? I can make a spectacle of poor old Fluffy, that's for sure. Claws and all!

"Have you gotten someone pregnant? I can reverse that for you, in a way you've probably never dreamed of. A few slices, a yank or two, and *goodbye unwanted responsibility!*"

"I'm sorry," Jonas said to the visitor. "This just isn't going to happen. Now if you'll excuse me..." Jonas moved the door closer to being closed, but Dr. Damage slipped his knee into the gap between door and doorframe.

"Oh, sir, please wait! I haven't even told you about my specials! Right now, this month only, it's two-for-one on rapes. What do you say? I've got half-off on all genital mutilations as well, provided you pay for at least one of each gend—"

Dr. Damage cut himself off abruptly, realizing that he no longer had Jonas' full attention. He turned sideways slowly, keeping his eyes on Jonas' eyes, until he was able to see where they were focused.

Jonas' attention had shifted across the street. He was scanning the block, house by house, seemingly in great detail, as if he had telescopic vision. His expression had changed to one of concern.

"As I was saying, sir, it's half-off genital mutilations right now, as long as..."

But Jonas wasn't hearing a word of it. Instead, he was focused on the red splatter on the door of the home directly across from his own. And the shattered windows on the house next to that. And the black soot surrounding the door and window frames of the next home. And the fact the next house down the line wasn't even there, but instead lay in a pile of splinters and rubble. Jonas wondered how had he failed to notice these details before.

And then it became clear why he had never encountered a single neighbor nor heard a single voice in all the time he'd lived there. There was only one answer, and it was a simple one. They were all dead. And in his estimation, at this particular moment, there could be only one person responsible for such locally concentrated carnage. Dr. Damage was to blame.

"...truly, sir—'The Human Puzzle' is one of my most extravagant options. It comes with a fair price tag, of course, but I'm certain you'll appreciate the craft involved, and you'll be absolutely thrilled with the results."

Jonas refocused, and locked eyes with the stranger on his doorstep.

"Well, sir?" Dr. Damage asked again. "Shall we proceed with some violence?"

Jonas snapped back into the moment. He grabbed the knob, whipping the door toward himself, then threw it forward. The edge of the thick wooden slab slammed into Dr. Damage's knee, crunching softly into him. The sound made by the impact reminded Jonas of biting into a not-quite-ripe peach. The man on the receiving end of the blow, however, didn't make a sound.

Jonas pulled the door back an inch as Damage retracted his leg, then he slammed the door shut, and threw the locks, securing himself inside. He braced his hands against the upper part of the door anyway, and stood there for a moment.

He heard nothing from the other side of the door. He brought his eye up to the peephole slowly, attempting to move in complete silence, although he suddenly wondered to himself why it mattered.

Jonas saw nothing outside. The porch was completely empty. Where had Dr. Damage gone? Surely he couldn't have run too far in a matter of seconds with a banged up knee.

Jonas' heart was pounding. He focused on his breathing, trying not to pant too loudly.

"My name...sir...is Dr. Damage." Jonas' entire body tensed up, and a tiny sound escaped his throat. He heard a deep breath from the other side of the door too.

"This is my name, as well as my occupation, as well as my way of life. And no one—especially not someone like you, good sir—is going to stand in the way of that."

Jonas peeled his hands off the door, and took a smooth step backward.

"I came here selling violence today," Dr. Damage continued, "and while it seems you're not interested in *buying...*" He paused for dramatic effect. "I've decided I'm certainly going to *make you pay.*"

Jonas continued moving backward, but kept his eyes on the door. There was light coming through the gap at the bottom, but it disappeared a second later, as Dr. Damage did something very quickly to blot it out. There was silence, then the door began to creak in its frame, straining against something.

A moment passed, then Jonas saw the black, sludge-like mass seeping through. It looked like crude oil and bread dough, and it was quickly squeezing its way into the house under the door.

He nearly tripped over his own feet backing away from the fast-expanding blob. Within seconds, it was the size of a cat, then a calf, then a car. Soon it was completely inside, and it heaved as if it was breathing.

It reconfigured itself, and stretched into a more vertical form, now looking like a black, bumpy, oblong balloon. Like a giant prune.

A seam appeared, a bit above center. It spoke.

"That's right, good sir. It's time to pay."

A pair of tendrils sprouted from the top half of the sludgy mass, above the mouth-seam, and crawled outward in opposite directions. They curled back upon themselves, resembling a certain door-to-door salesman's mustache.

Then a dozen tentacles shot out from the body of the thing, all in the direction of Jonas. He dashed toward the steps, and up, avoiding the many arms of the amorphous thing that had just entered his home.

He ran upstairs, and the thing followed. It slurped its way up the steps, a few tentacles grabbing the railing to help along the way. When it reached the top, Jonas was nowhere to be found, and the doors to every room were closed.

The bathroom faced the top of the steps. The black sludge-thing stood tall again, facing the door, then shrank down a bit and changed form again, solidifying itself in the form of a man, about six and a half feet tall, wearing a formal pinstriped suit and a bowler hat. His mustache looked less like hair, and more like a pair of black tendrils sprouting from his face—a face with a wide-eyed expression, and a curious lack of eyebrows.

"Ohhh *sirrr?*" Dr. Damage announced, as he knocked on the bathroom door. "I believe we have some business to attend to."

The door shot open, revealing Jonas in a battle stance, brandishing a red rubber plunger with a wooden handle.

"Oh, hello there," he said, matter-of-factly.

Dr. Damage lunged forward, mustache first. But Jonas was faster, and he slammed the door on him, bouncing the salesman backward. He tumbled back down the staircase, but didn't make a sound.

Jonas ran down after him, plunger still in hand. On the way, he saw a tiny blur out of the corner of his eye, along the baseboard. He remembered, again, that he needed to buy mousetraps, then cursed himself for losing focus.

At the bottom of the stairs, Dr. Damage did a backwards somersault, then stood upright.

"Oh, I do detest pro bono work," he said, dusting off his shoulders. "But...the work *must* be done. And at least I can say that I truly love what I do."

Jonas leapt from the fourth step, landing his foot in Dr. Damage's chest. It stuck for a second, then he found his footing on the hardwood floor. A gooey, black wound appeared on the salesman's chest, as if his body and his clothing were both hurt.

Jonas gave a swift sideways kick, knocking Damage's feet out from under him. It was easier than he expected, and the stranger fell in a heap. From there, Jonas began to pound, and stomp, and kick. He dropped to the floor himself, serving up knees and elbows, and pokes with the plunger handle. With each strike, Dr. Damage bruised, dark and oily. He turned soft, and soon, he was nothing more than a ball of slick black dough, about the size of a volleyball.

Jonas pierced the mass with the handle of the plunger, and lifted it. He walked down the hall to the first floor bathroom, and dropped the sludge-thing into the toilet. He plunged and plunged. Then he flushed.

"Music to my ears," he whispered to himself.

●

A half hour later, Jonas was in the kitchen, finally pouring himself a cup of coffee. The plunger stood in the trash can, propping up the hinged lid.

As he took his first sip, a familiar blur dashed along the baseboard. Another ran past the refrigerator. Both quickly disappeared. Jonas sighed.

"Okay, you little buggers. Where are you hiding?" Jonas set his coffee mug on the counter and turned to stalk the mice.

There was silence for a moment, then he heard rustling from beneath the radiator. He moved in that direction carefully, ready for either or both of the mice to dart out and make a run for it.

And then they did. But they weren't mice. And instead of running away, they leapt up at Jonas. He wasn't expecting to be attacked. He certainly wasn't expecting Dr. Damage's eyebrows to attach themselves to his forehead.

Jonas fell down, knocked over by the force of the strange, living clusters of hair, and passed out.

When he woke up, he was amused to find that he was now wearing a formal suit, and a bowler hat. He picked himself up off the floor, brushed himself off, and tugged at one of the curls of his mustache, which must have grown in while he was sleeping.

"Well then," he said. "I suppose I'm back in business. Time to go make some sales."

Wrecking Ball

I didn't see the wrecking ball until approximately half a second before it hit my face.

You might think a spherical object wouldn't have slicing power, but you'd be wrong. That wrecking ball took my head off. Clean. The fact that I had burrowed my feet into the sand probably helped.

When I woke up, everything was black. I wondered whether I was now a head without a body, or a body without a head. I thought about a movie I saw once that asked this same sort of question. I thought about a song that sampled those very lines of dialogue.

I wished I could see something. But one of two things was true: Either my body no longer had eyes to see with, or that wrecking ball had smashed my eyes shut for good.

The fact that I could hear doctors discussing my situation made me think I was a head.

The fact that I felt hungry made me think I was a body.

The fact that I could smell antiseptic made me think I was a head.

The fact that I could feel tingling sensations in my fingers and toes made me think I was a body.

The fact that I was thinking any of these things made me think I was a head.

"He may never be able to walk again," they said. "He may never be able to see again," they also said.

Finally, after what seemed like forever, I was taken to surgery. I was there for hours. They may have put me under. I assume that was the case, but so much has been up in the air. I remember needles and scalpels and lasers and seagulls and a small golden retriever drinking a tiny cup of green tea while sitting on a giant ear of blue corn.

When the surgery was finished, I woke up to find myself in a recovery room. A nurse was sitting beside the bed, reading a newspaper. The light in the room was dim, my vision made even dimmer by the layers of gauze wrapped around me.

But I could see!

"Just a minute, dear," the nurse said, standing up from the chair. She left for a few seconds, then returned with a doctor.

"You've been through quite an ordeal," the doctor said as he walked through the door. "You'll need to continue resting, of course, but it's good you're awake."

The nurse raised the bed slowly, as the doctor leaned in toward me. He grabbed a pair of scissors and snipped at the gauze, then began to unravel my vision. It took several minutes, but I was able to see more with each passing second.

Finally I could see everything again. I looked down at my body, wrapped in a white hospital gown and covered in a blue polka-dotted sheet.

I looked at the nurse, confused, perhaps still foggy from whatever they used to put me under. Her head was a seagull.

I turned toward the doctor. His head was an ear of corn.

"It's important to breathe, dear," the nurse said.

"What you're about to see may shock you," said the doctor.

Then the nurse took me by the arm, and led me to the bathroom. When I looked in the mirror, I saw what they meant. My head was now a wrecking ball. The very one that hit me.

"Now, I'm afraid I must be leaving," said the doctor. "Please get your rest. Nurse, I'll see you at the beach."

The seagull-headed nurse nodded, still holding my arm.

I tried to scream, but wrecking balls don't make any noise unless they hit something.

I smashed my face into the mirror.

Playtime

She's nearly two knuckles in, the left side of her face scrunched into a picture of pain. When she extracts her finger from the nostril, there's a tiny alien rock formation attached to it.

"Ugh...I wish I had nails," she says.

She smashes the booger between her thumb and index finger, and rolls the yellow-green mass into a ball. Then she squishes it into a tiny pancake, and places it on the game board.

"Nice move," says her brother, from the other side of the table. "But check this out."

He rolls up his sleeve, peels a scab from his elbow, and places it on a vacant square. He leans back in his chair and smiles.

"Whatever," says the sister. She rolls her eyes, then rubs the corner of one of them, and produces a chunk of crust that's been seated there all morning. She places it on the board next to the scab.

The brother digs a pinky into his ear canal, and removes a ball of gummy brown wax. He sticks it to a corner space.

"Take *that*," he says.

The sister squints and puckers the corner of her mouth, then removes a shoe and sock, and scrapes at the space between her fourth and fifth toes, until she has enough soft cheese for a play, and uses it to block her brother's move. Both of their expressions change. She giggles.

He reaches through the neck of his shirt, and yanks a skin tag from under his arm. He sets it down.

She hocks up a ball of phlegm. He peels off a fingernail. She slices open a vein, and dribbles on the game board. He pulls something brown with a hair stuck in it from the back of his pants. She grabs a pair of pliers and pulls out a canine tooth. He unzips, and pisses onto the center of the board. She snaps off her own thumb, and drops it in the puddle.

Then he grabs a giant, colorful feather from somewhere, and violently stabs it, quill first, into the center of the only open square left. There's a pause in the room, as the dust settles, and the sister's jaw slowly drops.

"Waaaaait a seconnnnd!" she screams, jumping to her feet, kicking back her chair. She grabs the corners of the table, and stares down at the board. Then she raises her eyes to meet his. "What the hell?! You dirty! Rotten! Filthy! Fucking! *Cheater!*"

Then she whips out a gun, and shoots him in the face.

Cat Tree Summer

After what feels like an hour, we finally reach a clearing in the woods. My hands and arms are all scraped up from pushing the branches and bushes aside, but I've been assured it will all be worth it. I hope so. Among other things, I need to get back to the cabin and make another attempt to write.

That was the idea for the summer, after all—spend a few months in the middle of nowhere and get some writing done. That was the plan, at least. It hasn't worked out too well, though. Hopefully my next sit-down will be more fruitful than the last seventeen.

My woodland guide, a three-headed talking dragonfly named Dino, first got my attention by buzzing in the air directly in front of my nose. I was taking a break from not getting any writing done. I swatted at him a few times, but he was far too quick for me.

"C'mon," he said. "I got somethin' t'show yuh."

So I followed. I'm not sure why. Boredom may have been a factor.

"*Dere* it is," he tells me now, using all three of his mouths in choral unison. He motions to the center of the clearing with his skinny legs, as if I can't tell what he wants me to look at.

"*Seriously?* You brought me here to look at a tree?" I ask him, as my eyebrows creep further and further up my forehead. "You led me through the woods—through *trees*—for an hour, to come look at another tree?"

I have to admit, it was an interesting-looking tree. But I had writing to do, and there were plenty of trees around.

"Trust me," says the dragonfly. "I never let yuh down before, did I?"

"We just met. Like an hour ago," I respond.

"So what? Go lookit the friggin tree."

So I step into the clearing. The soles of my shoes crunch down on the gray sand-and-gravel mixture that seems incredibly out of place in the otherwise lush scenery of these woods. In the center of the dry patch is a single, oddly-shaped tree, much shorter and wider in it's reach than anything else I've encountered in the woods so far. It's black, with dozens of smoothly curled limbs that seem to be bearing some even more oddly-shaped, oddly-colored fruit.

There's a soft, rhythmic rumbling in the distance. For a second, I worry about getting caught in rain on the way back, but the thought quickly disappears from my mind.

I make my way closer to the tree, and I can see that its bark isn't actually bark at all. It's more like fur—a coat of shiny black that shimmers with the light breeze that sweeps through every now and then.

When I get close enough to touch it, I do. I run my hand along the trunk of the weird tree, petting it like an animal, and I notice that the rumbling sound I heard a minute ago is louder. I notice the trunk expanding and contracting, just slightly, and I feel a vibration coming from within. The tree is breathing. The tree is...*purring*.

"It's a cat tree. Y'ever seen one?"

I don't even bother responding.

"Yeah, didn't think so."

There's a knot on the trunk with a dot of yellow at its center, and for a second I feel like I'm being watched. I've always felt that way about tree knots, though. They've always looked like eyes to me. That's why I can't stand hardwood floors.

I keep petting the unusual tree, and start thinking about its story potential. In the back of my mind is the fact that I need to get back to the cabin and do some work, but I really don't want to leave. I glance over at Dino, and he winks at me with three of his six eyes.

The tree stops purring, which steals my attention back. Of course my eyes go right back to the knot, just in time to see it start to quiver. Then, suddenly, it expands, and produces a trio of yellow turds, which it promptly drops at my feet. I make a sound I couldn't possibly spell, and jump back. The tree starts purring again.

"Well?" says Dino. "Yuh gonna try one, or what?"

"What? You've got to be kidding me."

"Not the turds, y'idiot. *The fruit!*"

I look up from the base of the tree, where I'm able to get a better look at the fruit. From a distance, they were partially obscured by the twisting black limbs, but up close I can see everything better. There are dozens of unusually-shaped masses—some gray, some pink, some a bit of both. Each has five or six appendages of varying sizes.

They all look like cats. Hairless cats, each about the size of a pineapple, each dangling from a furry branch by its tail, swaying softly, like fleshy pendulums in the breeze, which has just now begun to pick up.

MMRRAOOOWW

The sound startles me. I feel my body tense up.

"Ooh, on your left! The pink one!" shouts Dino, so quickly he nearly stumbles over his own words. *"Geddit!"*

"What are you talking about?" I say. I shoot a confused look in the direction of the talking dragonfly.

"The pink one on your left! They meow when they're ripe!"

I look back up, and realize the one he's talking about seems to be wriggling a bit, and not just swaying in the wind. Its features seem a bit more defined, though I wouldn't say it has a face. It looks more like a cat made of wax, perhaps heated up a bit, just to smooth out the edges.

I move closer to it, and realize I can reach it if I get up on my toes. So I do. With both hands, I pull at the cat fruit, stretching the limb it's attached to downward, until the hairless object snaps free from the tree's fur-lined appendage. The fruit moves a bit in my hands, but doesn't seem to want to get away. On the contrary, it seems completely comfortable in my grasp.

So I take a bite.

The skin is easy to pierce, and I'm happy to find that the cat fruit is boneless. It's flesh is soft and juicy, sweet and delicious, like a peach. I devour it quickly, each bite better than the last, and I discover a very simple cat-shaped pit at the fruit's center, which, strangely enough, looks like a cookie. I resist the urge to bite into it for a second, but it looks like a ginger snap to me, and I can't stop myself. I love ginger snaps.

Unfortunately the pit tastes more like black licorice, which I can't stand, so I drop it from my tongue to my hand.

"What are yuh doin'? That's the best part!"

I've had about enough of Dino's accent. I'm just about to throw the pit at him, when—

MMRRAOOOOOWWW

It's another ripe one. This one's pink as well, but two different shades marbled together. It's bigger and even more delicious than the first, and I finish it in half the time.

There's a tingling sensation in the back of my brain. Something familiar, but lost. Not ancient, but old. I recognize it, and suddenly feel the need to race back to the cabin and write.

MMRRAOOOWW...MMMMRRAAOOOOOO-WWWW...MMRRAOOOWW

It's as if I have a new addiction, and the tree is responding with the fix. A chorus of ripening fruit sings out loud, and I find myself jumping up and down, snatching each cat-shaped piece as they call to me. I can't keep up. They start falling to the ground on their own. And then—

There's a deep rumble in the distance. I think it's thunder at first, then realize it sounds more like the purring of the cat tree. It begins rhythmically, but quickly becomes a drone, then gets louder. And louder. The limbs of the cat tree and the gravel beneath us begin to shake, and I think it's an earthquake. Suddenly, the tree and the entire clearing surrounding it start to grow, like a small mountain rising up out of the landscape. The gravel rolls away in all directions, and I wrap my arms around the cat tree trunk to keep from losing my balance. The other trees surrounding everything fall backward, bending away from the cat tree and I. In the chaos, I lose track of Dino the dragonfly.

Seconds later, all the gravel has fallen away, revealing a landscape that matches the tree. The ground is covered in a thick black fur, and it heaves as if it's breathing.

Because it is.

With the gravel gone now, I can see what's going on. The cat tree is attached to the ground, and the ground is actually a giant mutant cat, which was buried beneath the dirt. The tree seems to be some sort of growth—something like a cyst, I guess. But I don't know too much about cysts. I don't know too much about mutant cat monsters either, but here we are.

It stands up and shakes me from the tree-thing on its back, and I fall to the wooded area below. Unhurt, I jump up and start to run. The massive feline thing chases me into the woods, and I haven't gotten very far by the time it swipes at me, knocks me into a bush, and then laps me up into its enormous mouth. Everything goes black.

●

"So how's this one comin' along?"

"Uh...pretty well, actually. Give me another half hour, and the first draft should be done. Then we'll eat."

It's been two months now, and the words have never come so easily.

Dino and I have made a fairly nice home for ourselves here inside the belly of the giant mutant fruiting cat. Overall, I'd say it's been a pretty great summer. Not too hot, either.

Something in the cat's stomach lining seems to glow, which is helpful. It's not overly bright—just enough that we can see what we're doing.

Apparently when the thing snatched the two of us up a couple months ago, it swallowed a few oak trees in the process—which turned out to be pretty lucky for us. We've been able to use the wood to fashion some furniture, crude as it may be.

And, luckily, the fruit grows on the inside too, so we've been using that for sustenance. I eat the fruit, and Dino eats the pits.

We've been fine.

I've been writing a lot—which was my plan for the summer all along. I'm doing a few stories a week, actually, using the notepad I had stashed in my pocket.

Fall is coming, though, and I need to start thinking about getting out of here and heading home. Dino doesn't seem to care either way, but he says he has a few ideas.

Maybe we'll start talking about that tomorrow. I'd like to finish what I'm working on now, then have a little something to eat.

Sweets

The long, cylindrical ones they make balloon animals out of? Those are perfect. Stick a few together if you need the length, and stuff them down in the belly. No—lower.

Some cotton candy next. Just press it down a bit and compress it into a nice soft oblong shape. Do two, actually. Use them for the lungs.

Kidneys, liver, etc. I don't know. See what you've got in the cabinets.

For the heart, a giant gummy bear, of course. You have to special-order those most of the time, but occasionally you can find them in candy shops. There should be one in the pantry. If not, just get a couple handfuls of the small ones, and we'll press 'em all together.

Red vines for veins. Makes sense, right? You've got to be careful with the placement, though. It's a whole complicated network, and you've got to get it right.

Once you have the insides done, drizzle some cherry syrup on everything, and close him up. Black licorice whips are great for that. Seal up that Y-incision nice and tight. Good.

That patch of skin that's missing? A piece of that fruit leather should work just fine there. I loved that stuff as a kid. You might need a second piece, but I doubt it.

Gumballs for eyes. Those flatter ones for teeth. I forget what they're called.

And a big popcorn ball too. Perfect for the brain. Just slide it in there, maybe spritz some of that soda around the perimeter, then put his cap back on, and roll his face back into place.

Okay, a few more stitches...and there you go! Well done!

We'll cast the spell tonight after dessert, and as long as we did everything right, he should rise by midnight.

But remember, we'll only have him 'til the sun comes up. When dawn breaks, he's sure to run off and join the circus. They always do.

Hole

"Put a damn shirt on," she says. It's about all she's said to me for the last twelve hours.

"Shut up," I say in response, too quiet for her to actually hear. I head into the kitchen and find myself staring blankly into the fridge several moments later, hungry for something that doesn't seem to be there.

I shut the door and stand in the middle of the room, not quite sure what I want to do next. My head is fuzzy, and I'm deeply, fundamentally tired. I check the fridge again, but still nothing looks good.

She comes in from the den, with a plate full of bones in one hand, bobbing in time with her steps and the smoldering cigarette dangling from her lips. There's a crash as she drops the plate into the sink, and the remains of whatever she just ate scatter themselves randomly around the basin. I look up, realizing I've been staring at a dust bunny in the corner of the room for a while, and flash her a look.

"What the hell is wrong with you today?" she asks.

I don't respond at all this time. She looks me up and down, and squints as she takes a pull from her smoke, then pops her lips open, and shakes her head disapprovingly before exhaling.

"Put a fucking shirt on already. It's disgusting," she says, before choking on the cloud hovering around her head.

And suddenly she's disappeared from the room, and I'm left standing there, wondering what she meant. Sure, I've put on a few pounds in the last month or two—but "disgusting"?

And then it hits me, quite literally. Her hand, then her wrist, then her arm up to the elbow, slide out of my chest, slicked wet with what I can only assume is my blood.

"You see? This is what I'm talking about!" she yells, right into my ear. "Now will you please put a goddamn shirt on?"

I look down at myself, completely bewildered—though I feel no pain—staring at the massive wound I've been carrying around for who knows how long. Standing behind me, she thrusts her arm in and out of it in a vaguely sexual manner, and I'm more than a little grossed out, not to mention physically shaken.

She extracts her arm, and circles around me, then flicks her cigarette into the sink and spits on the wall. She wipes my blood on her pants as she exits the room.

And I find myself standing there again, just staring, thinking, dazed. I hear her coughing again from the other room.

And it occurs to me that she's right. This is disgusting. I should show a little consideration. I head to the other room, to find a shirt.

Drive

The crashed car undid itself. Twisted metal unfolded, jagged edges smoothed, bent lines straightened. Patches of rust effervesced into the air and disappeared.

I reached for the driver's side door handle, now shiny-new, and pulled. I sank down into the bucket seat, which seemed to somehow sit lower than the pavement beneath the tires.

The woman in the passenger seat was some sort of punk-jock hybrid. Black smears under her eyes. Multi-colored pigtails hanging at a dozen angles. Shoulder pads. Elbow pads. Safety pin in her lip. A torn jersey, oversized, with the number 99 on it. Yellow lipstick that seemed to glow, reflecting some unknown light source.

Upon closer inspection, I realized the smears on her cheeks were actually a pair of very detailed line drawings of tiny cars. Hot rods. Maybe tattooed there.

"Drive," she said.

The spider web cracks in the windshield erased themselves, and I could see the surf racing toward us. From between the buildings, a wave of purple-gray water rushed in our direction, foaming pink along the edges like a chemical spill.

A kid on a dirt bike was wheelie-riding the crest of it, waving a severed, cherry-colored tentacle in the air above his head. His body language was telling us to go. *Go now.*

The car was already running. I popped it into reverse and checked the rearview on instinct. A pair of chimps sat nervously in the back seat, trapped in place by harnesses, cages with sensors wrapped around their heads. They were clearly distressed, but remained silent. I hadn't noticed them until now. They locked eyes with my reflection.

"Drive! Drive! Drive!" the kid screamed.

I hit the gas, and spun the car backwards in an arc, then slammed on the brakes, moved the needle back to D, and gunned it. In the mirror, I spotted the kid between the chimps' heads, pedaling furiously on the water. He dropped his front wheel and tossed the tentacle at us. It helicoptered through the air, landed on the trunk, and stuck there.

The water behind us seemed to grow taller as the buildings receded in the distance. Ahead, I spotted a bridge. I knew if I could just make it there before the water reached us, everything would be fine.

"Drive! Drive! Drive!" my punk-jock companion yelled, slapping her palms on the dashboard with each word. The chimps started panting, showing their panic.

I gripped the steering wheel as hard as I could and stood on the gas pedal. We raced toward the bridge, hitting the entrance just a moment later. The car bucked as we began climbing the span, and the purple wave behind us crashed around the foot of it, bleeding into the river beneath us.

The woman beside me screamed, excited, but the chimps in the back looked no more relaxed. The kid on the bike had disappeared. I was pretty sure he drowned. The tentacle on the trunk was wagging in the wind like a tail.

And then, as we reached the middle point of the bridge, it gave out. The center of the structure just ahead of us crumbled and fell into the water below. We launched off one ragged end, into the air, and hung there, floating like some cartoon bad guy before recognizing the existence of gravity.

We're still hanging here, floating like a metal cloud between the two broken stubs of a formerly functional bridge. But the chimps no longer seem concerned.

Horns Up

Damon's right at the front, fist in the air, horns up, banging his head like a madman. Like a bobblehead doll in an earthquake. Like his neck is a Slinky. The music courses through his veins. It burns, but that's a good thing.

The band on stage, the one whose logo looks like a pile of kindling, is playing music from their latest album. They believe it may be their greatest work yet, and Damon agrees. He's got the vinyl picture disc at home, resting as the centerpiece in the shrine he's created. The one his parents don't know about. The one he's got hidden away in his closet, tucked behind his clothes, all of them black.

Behind him, the people in the pit are spinning and bouncing, slamming into each other, circling endlessly. They move like laundry in a dryer. They surge forward occasionally, waves of flesh and denim crashing toward the stage. Sweaty leather presses into Damon, forcing him into the barrier, pushing him even closer to his heroes standing five feet taller than him. He doesn't mind.

Looking up, he sees them shred, sees their heads bobbing in unison, keeping time with the frenetic beat, like pom-poms in the hands of heavily-caffeinated cheerleaders.

Their sweat rains down, occasionally splashing his face. He thinks of it as a sort of communion. He waits for Killem, the guitarist with the sunken eyes, to flip a pick into the crowd, hoping it will land softly, delicately on his tongue.

The staccato growls emanating from Grindface, the vocalist, reverberate inside Damon too. They scrape his insides, slowly gutting him, removing anything that isn't necessary at this moment in time. Cleansing him.

The drum kit sits atop a massive sculpture, the head of something demonic, with horns sprouting in two directions. Cymbals are perched on each of them. An evil grin displays giant pointed teeth, and motors make it move. Smoke leaks out at very specific moments of the performance. And small orange fires glow inside the eyes, flickery but constant throughout the show.

The lights above the stage flicker too, and shift and burst, like a psychedelic storm above the band. Like lightning is striking them, enhancing their energy. Fueling them.

It fuels the crowd too, but none moreso than Damon. He's still standing against the barrier, banging his head with the music, arm still raised, horns up in salute.

Now the band on stage, the band whose logo looks like someone dropped a bail of hay from a skyscraper, is belting out a song they've never played live before. Damon feels the music. It speaks to him in a way his mother's voice never could.

He still has his arm raised high, horns up, when something happens. The guitars squeal in some unholy harmony, high-pitched and piercing. The lights strobe violently.

Damon's hand, the one he's held tall all night, the one that's a half-fist with two fingers extended, starts to transform. The skin on the two straight digits begins to melt like wax on a burning candle. The flesh drips down, falling from the bone, just as the fingers start to grow even longer. They extend into a pair of sharp, calcified points. Horns.

The flesh on the two central fingers begins to soften as well, and the fingers fuse to each other. Underneath them, from the concealed palm of Damon's hand, a pair of eyes reveal themselves. They glow orange, like embers, from their cores.

Damon's thumb expands and mutates, bending until it becomes a rigid jawline. A pointed row of teeth grows out of it, meshing with the bottom edge of the fused fingers.

His fist now has a face, something demonic, made of twisted flesh and reformed bone. Horns up.

The jaw sprouts a small triangle of hair from what used to be a knuckle, a tiny pointed beard, and the head begins to bob furiously in time with the music. A strip of flesh peels itself away and hangs over the edge, a ragged, red, forked tongue.

Seconds later, ridges begin to rise along the back of Damon's wrist. A dozen small, bony protrusions form, pushing out from the flesh like hardened pimples. They trail down his arm as the skin bubbles and stretches in every direction.

Other, more linear ridges form on the inside of his forearm. A ribcage. Below, the muscles expand and contract, as the thing his arm is becoming begins to breathe on its own.

The elbow grows into a razor-edged tail. It wags back and forth, like that of an excited dog. But this is something much different. Much meaner.

Damon's arm stretches further, like he's giving birth to something from his shoulder. It never breaks away completely, though. It's part of him, a bulbous balloon of evil, a living ventriloquist's puppet he could never put down.

The music doesn't stop. If anything, it grows louder and louder, faster and faster. The double bass drum beat becomes a constant drone, the guitars scream a wall of distorted noise.

The lighting rigs above the stage explode, showering everything with a rainstorm of white sparks, while the walls of the club, once firm stone, start to crack. They crumble from the top down, in a spiral path of physical destruction that works its way quickly to the cement below.

The floor, sticky from beer and who knows what else, breaks open under the still-raging crowd. A light as bright as the sun shows through the cracks. Soon the surface is all just rocks. The pit of swirling concertgoers slide down into the pool of lava bubbling beneath the crumbles.

The demon sculpture under the drum set begins to laugh maniacally, along with the thing Damon's arm has become. A wave of heat erupts from the hole in the ground, and the band members turn to vapor and dust on impact. Somehow, the music, now just static, doesn't seem to stop.

Damon is still standing there, banging his head, horns up. Finally, the demon-thing that sprouted from his shoulder breaks free, tears itself from its meaty bonds, and turns toward its host. Damon's head stops for a moment, and the monster's glowing eyes meet his. They laugh at each other just before the beast lunges in, baring its mighty fangs, and then sinking them into what's left of Damon.

And even as he's being devoured, he never stops smiling.

We Built the Moon

Long ago, we built the moon. We just needed something to do, so that's what we did.

The most difficult part was getting there. Eventually, we built a very tall ladder, which we braced at the bottom with sandbags, and we climbed. We climbed a very long way.

We used what we had to build the moon—namely, wood and nails.

One of my colleagues, a dairy farmer, suggested we use cheese, as he had more than enough readily available. But I reminded him that cheese was not an Approved Building Material, and that was that. We ate some of the cheese instead.

Then we built. We used every scrap of wood we could get our hands on. There were planks discarded by the lumber yard, and logs from Old Man Witherby's firewood collection. We used tree stumps and park benches and pieces of the clubhouse that used to belong to that poor boy who died from tuberculosis. There was driftwood from the beach. Even an old barn door.

We cut everything into odd shapes and nailed it all together until it resembled, more or less, something big and round and pockmarked hanging in the nighttime sky. We lit it with a spotlight. It didn't have to be perfect, and it wasn't. From a distance, no one would know the difference.

Then, a long time ago—but in the grand scheme of things, not really that long ago at all—it was announced that some other people were going to take a trip to the moon.

So we had to go back before them, and clean things up a bit. We sanded down the corners and smoothed the edges. We tightened screws, set nails, filled in gaps with spackle, laid in drywall, and gave everything a few coats of paint.

We finished just in time to get back home and see our handiwork on the television. It looked pretty good, if I do say so myself.

I don't expect we'll have to go back again anytime soon, but you never know. We've got plenty of cheese, just in case.

The Bigot

The Bigot wakes up one morning, early, without the aid of his alarm.

He struggles to see in the early morning darkness. His eyes are still practically glued shut, and he can't remember where he left his glasses. He half-heartedly reaches for them, but they aren't in the usual spot.

He decides to fall back to sleep. He rolls over. His legs are tangled in the sheet, but he's too exhausted to care.

His arm and shoulder are sore, perhaps from the way he slept on them. His jaw hurts too. Maybe he was grinding his teeth again. He puts the pain out of his mind, and burrows the other side of his face into the other half of the pillow.

Thunder crashes in the distance, and the room fills with flickering light. At the same moment, a loud buzzer sounds. The Bigot jolts completely awake and sits straight up, sideways on the bed.

Mounted on the wall, high above the bed, near the ceiling, is a red light inside a wire cage. It begins to spin and flash.

The Bigot's eyes adjust, and he realizes something. This is not his bedroom. This is not his house.

His glasses are gone, but he's able to see well enough. He frees his legs from the covers and climbs off the bed to go examine his surroundings. The floor beneath his feet is concrete, and cool.

With each step, the Bigot feels electric shocks of pain, and sore extremities. His arms and hands throb. His legs ache. His feet feel swollen, as if he is walking on inflated balloons.

At the far end of the room, a full-length mirror hangs on the wall. As he makes his way to it, the Bigot passes several tables filled with strange-looking metal tools. In addition to the unrecognizable implements, he sees knives, saws, pliers, spools of wire and thread, and so on. There are large cylindrical tanks with hoses running in and out of them. There are white cloths thrown in piles, stained with dark red splotches. There are probably twenty gurneys.

The Bigot approaches the mirror. He is wearing a long hospital gown, dull and dingy from age. It's an older style. He tugs at the ties until it falls from his body.

And just like that, he sees the truth. He sees the stitches. His body, once uniformly pale and pasty, is now a colorful mosaic.

The Bigot examines his reflection.

He sees mismatched patches of flesh sewn together. He sees various body parts of all different sizes, proportions, and colors. He sees light and dark browns, muted burgundies, olive tones. He sees pale yellows, and peaches, and pinks. There are thatches of thick, curly dark hair, areas with thin layers of fine blonde, and other places where the hair has been completely removed. He sees decades-old scars, a scattering of tattoos both crisp and blurry, and several relatively new piercings. It is all so unfamiliar, and yet it is all now a part of him.

He turns around so he can look over his shoulder, and view the road map on his back. He catches a glimpse of a small pink breast hanging beneath his armpit on his left side, and wonders why he didn't notice it from the front. He sees two buttocks of different colors, then turns back around.

His face is not the one he remembers. His eyes are different colors now—one brown, one blue. He pulls bandages from the top of his head, and his hair flops forward. He combs it back with his fingers to reveal a prominent arc of stitching across his forehead.

The Bigot continues to gaze into the mirror as lightning flashes once again outside, illuminating the room with blue-white light to compete with the red over the bed.

The Bigot stares into his new eyes as the intercom crackles into the room. He hears dozens of people's voices, and they are all laughing. Laughing at him.

Thunder crashes again.

The Bigot screams.

The Pet

The dog, out for a walk, just before squatting for a shit by a tree, exploded at the end of its leash. Flesh split, organs burst, fluids splattered, ropes of intestines jumped through the air like wet party streamers.

The dog's owner was surprised. None of his pets had ever exploded before. He stood there, mouth agape, then looked up and down the street to see if anyone else had noticed. But there was no one else around.

Half a minute later, the various pieces of animal started to reassemble. All the internal parts converged, while chunks of meat, some covered with patches of fur, crawled toward each other.

Soon the dog was a dog again. Only now it was a cow.

The owner was confused. He bent down to look underneath the dog, and examined the dog's udder.

"Hmm," he said, tweaking one of the teats with his index finger. "I guess you really are a cow now, aren't you?"

"Yes," the cow said. "I mean...*mmmooooooo...*" Then the cow began sauntering down the street, with the owner following closely behind, his hand still on the leash.

Half a minute later, at an intersection, the cow exploded. It made a much louder sound than the dog had, and the owner once again looked around to see if any of his neighbors had seen what had happened. But like before, the owner and his exploded pet were alone on the street.

The pet pieces reformed again a half minute later, and the cow had become a cat.

The owner looked at his pet in disgust. He did not like cats. They reminded him of lions, and he *really* disliked lions. Then the cat said something in French.

The owner absolutely *hated* the French. His face immediately turned red, his body tensed, and he began to shake involuntarily.

Half a minute later, the owner exploded. The leash, now saturated with blood, dropped to the ground.

The cat glanced up and down the street quickly, then, one by one, approached the scattered pieces of the owner. It devoured everything quickly, not even bothering to chew everything completely. When it had finished, the cat sat back, content, and exploded.

Half a minute later, in the shadow of a stop sign, the cat parts slurped toward each other, smashed into each other, and attached themselves to each other. The cat, whole again, finally stood up on two legs, its form now human. The cat had become the owner.

The owner looked around. Seeing no one, he unbuckled the leash from his neck and tossed it behind a shrub. He rubbed the back of a hand across his cheek several times, then waited half a minute before walking home.

Slices of Me

It wasn't an easy decision. It wasn't something I took lightly. I understood the seriousness of all of it. As soon as I made the choice, I began making preparations.

I had a yard sale, and was able to get rid of most of my possessions that way. My neighbors were both confused and excited to see that it technically wasn't a sale, since I was giving everything away for free.

Yes, it's all here for the taking. No, I don't have pets. Yes, of course the blender works. No, I've never had bed bugs.

You like that ugly ship-in-a-bottle lamp? It's yours. You want those half-empty cans of paint? Take 'em. The area rug with the yin and yang design and the matching end tables? I'll help you load them in your truck.

Whatever I couldn't give away that weekend stayed in the yard until trash day, then went to the curb to get hauled off.

I quit my job the next day. I gave no notice. My boss was angry, but I could tell most of my coworkers were excited for me. They seemed to like that I screwed management over, since the following week began our busiest time of year. On my way out the door, many of the people I rarely, if ever, spoke to gave approving winks or nods. They would never do something so bold themselves, but they loved that someone else did.

I threw my ID badge in the trash can just outside the front door. I imagine my boss saw me do it from his window, but I didn't bother to look up. It didn't really matter to me one way or the other.

That night I drove into the city, and donated all my clothes to the homeless folks on the streets. All but what I was wearing, of course.

I gave them the food from my refrigerator too, and virtually everything from my cabinets. One man in particular got all the canned stuff, and I made sure to give him an opener too, despite the fact that he said he already had one. He produced it from his pocket, and I debated internally over what was on the tip—rust or blood.

When everything I had packed into my car had been doled out, I left the car itself near a central intersection, up for grabs to whoever was brazen enough to take it. I left the keys in the ignition, the doors unlocked, and the driver's side window down.

I walked home that night. The route I chose was a dangerous one—through a part of the city most people warn their loved ones about and stay away from themselves. Surprisingly, though, no one bothered me.

Upon returning home, I used the restroom, then went around the house to make sure my few remaining possessions were well organized. I also cracked several first floor windows open, then made my way to the kitchen.

I sat down in the only chair left, at a small folding table I had held onto. There, over the course of about half an hour, I wrote a letter, addressed to no one in particular, describing what had brought me to this point. After all, I may have had no family, but I knew my neighbors well, and I didn't want them to be left with any misconceptions or false stories.

I had simply reached an end point, and I wanted it all to be over.

I reached for the one kitchen implement I had kept behind—my trusty chef's knife. I stared at the blade, admiring the glint of the overhead light as I turned it, slowly, back and forth in my hand.

I was about to become one with that silver.

I rested an arm on the table, positioned so that my palm was up, and I sat forward in my chair. I brought the knife down firmly, and sliced across my wrist. I put some heft into the motion, figuring I wouldn't want to take a second swipe.

I was wrong. Wrong about everything. So very, very wrong.

The sharp edge of the knife broke the skin, but also sliced halfway through my arm. There was no blood, which surprised me—but even more shocking was the ease with which the blade passed through. It was like cutting into a hot dog.

I didn't feel the slightest bit of pain.

I raised my arm up, and my hand fell limp, opening the wound wider. I examined the cut, and found that the meat inside was of uniform color and texture. There was no bone. The cross section of my own arm reminded me of something akin to liverwurst, of all things.

I repeated the slicing motion with the knife, this time severing my hand completely from the arm. I was still surprised by the lack of blood, but upon examining the stump, I noticed several droplets of moisture starting to develop.

I set down the knife and picked up my hand to take a closer look. It felt soft. And, stranger still, there was a pleasant scent emanating from the open end.

The urge to taste the inside of my wrist hit me. That was as unexpected as anything, but at this point, I could think of no reason not to.

I slid the tip of my tongue along the end of my severed hand. It was delicious. I wanted more immediately, so I nibbled.

The flavor was indescribable. It was overwhelming. It was new and strange and nearly impossible to believe.

I took a larger bite, then another, and realized my heart was thumping hard. Adrenaline raced through me. I turned animalistic, like a predator perched over his kill, and in moments I had devoured the entire hand, swallowing each bite down with what I can only call a culinary euphoria.

I took a moment to breathe. Then I picked up the knife again.

I began slicing away at my arm like a machine. In just a few moments, I had transformed my arm into a staggered pile of eighth-inch thick medallions. There was still no blood, and no bone, and no pain.

The task made me salivate, seeing each perfect slice fall away from my arm, knowing what it tasted like. I stopped at the elbow and slipped a fresh slice of myself between my lips. Each bite was more delicious than the last. It was addictive.

I stuffed another piece into my mouth. It made my taste buds sing.

Then I stopped. I had to.

There are moments in life when ideas are shifted, priorities get rearranged, and entire worldviews flip upside down. This was one of those moments. Everything I had known up to that point suddenly changed with a taste of my own arm.

This was the greatest thing I had ever done. It felt wrong somehow to keep it all for myself. Others had to know. I had to share it. I had to bring it to the world.

I stood up from the table and searched the kitchen, but there was very little around. I needed a plate, or some sort of tray. I went through drawers and cabinets, even searched the oven and the spaces to either side of the refrigerator. But there was nothing to be found.

With my good arm, I tore the door off one of the cabinets. It took several pulls, and I had to adjust for my now-lopsided body weight, but I had enough strength to do it.

Placing the door down on the table, I gathered the stack of slices from my arm, and assembled them into two even rows, as if I was about to present a tray of hors d'ocuvies at a gala.

●

The next morning, I was back in the city, at the intersection where I left my car. The car had disappeared, of course, which made me smile.

Overnight, I had constructed a table from pieces of scrap wood and metal I found in a nearby alley. When people started to appear on the streets, on their way to work, I was ready for them.

SLICES OF ME, the sign in front of my table read. I had scratched the letters into a piece of a two-by-four, then rubbed dirt into the scratches, to make them more visible. It wasn't the greatest sign, but it seemed to bring a few people over. Some couldn't make out the words, so they asked.

My first few customers seemed skeptical at first, unsure of whether or not they should try a slice. I say customers, but again, I was offering my wares free of charge.

But as soon as the first brave individual tasted a piece of my arm, and fell to her knees, I was in business, so to speak. When the others in the small crowd that had gathered saw her reaction, they all wanted to try it for themselves.

I handed a slice to everyone who wanted one. I watched as they sniffed, then nibbled along the edge, before stuffing the entire piece into their mouths. I watched their eyes roll back, and the waves of pleasure pass through their bodies. Some people began jumping up and down. Others had to sit on the pavement. Some screamed out in jubilation, and called over to their friends, telling them they had to cross the street to try one of my slices.

For the first time in a long time, I was happy. I felt like I was doing what I was meant to do.

The hours passed, but my customers never stopped coming. They all wanted a piece of me, and I was happy to oblige. At a certain point, however, I had to start making each slice a bit thinner, as I only had so much to give. People understood the rarity of my product - but it seemed the restrictive quality of it only made the demand grow. Lines formed in two directions, each so long they disappeared in the distance.

It wasn't long before my arm and both legs were completely gone, devoured by the hungry public. I had to prop myself up on my makeshift table and find new angles from which to cut. Soon I was offering slices from my hips, and my shoulder, and then, eventually, my belly and back.

Before long, I had been reduced—quite willingly, mind you—to just a head and an arm. They remained connected by a small bit of flesh. I had sliced most of my neck away, and taken a good portion from my second shoulder.

I lay there on the table, marveling at my sudden popularity. I looked at the faces of the people standing before me, eager for a slice.

I had finally found a reason to live, but in the process, I had literally given myself away. Here I was, with a reason for being, but I was nearly gone. Once again, I had reached an end point.

I grasped my trusty chef's knife, and paused to think. Would the next slice come from my head, or from the arm doing the slicing? And what would come after that?

The crowd before me was growing impatient. I had a decision to make.

Brother Barry

Well would you look at that? As I live and breathe on this beautiful earth! Mama done sat right up in her casket and bit dear brother Barry on the neck! Shoot, I can't hardly believe it.

Kinda serves him right, though, dontcha think? I mean, I can't seem to figure out—not for the life of me—who put Barry in charge of this here funeral anyway. Doesn't make one dang bit of sense.

He didn't love Mama. No-sir-ee. Can't say he really liked her, even. And she sure didn't care too much for him neither. So how he ended up with this responsibility is really beyond me. And just look what he's done.

Ooh! She really took a big chunk outta his neck, didn't she? Got him good. *Lawdy.* Which reminds me, I need to put that roast in the oven the minute we get home. Don't let me forget, will you?

Well, Barry sure had the book-smarts all his life, you betcha. Even as a child, he was showing us all up at every turn. Perfect scores on every test, perfect grades on every report card. Perfect teeth too. But book smarts aren't everything. Bird-brained brother Barry didn't get a dang thing right about this funeral, and that's the honest truth.

For starters, Mama didn't even *want* a funeral with a casket! Nope. Everyone knew that. She wanted to be turned to ash—not buried. And she definitely didn't want a church service, that's for darn sure. But the preacher man's here, and so are we.

I just don't get it. Mama hated, I mean *hated* roses. So why's this room full of 'em? What was brother Barry thinking with that book-smart noggin of his?

Oh, she hated purple too. How could he not remember that? When we were kids, she used to hide the purple crayons, she hated that color so much! I don't even know whose dress that is they squeezed her into up there. Looks like somethin' someone picked up at that half-rate thrift shop down the road. Dang thing doesn't even fit right. 'Course it's stained somethin' horrible now too, what with all the blood, so that doesn't help matters.

And those white streaks in her hair—what's with that? They weren't there before. He musta had them funeral parlor people add 'em or somethin'. Makes her head look like a skunk, you ask me. And frankly, between you an' me, she probably smells like one right about now too. Dirty, rotten critters.

Golly, he sure is bleeding something fierce, ain't he? Is someone gonna mop that up? Somebody's liable to slip and break their dang neck. What kinda rinky-dink operation they runnin' here anyway?

That minister fella sure said some nice things about Mama, though, that's for certain. 'Course, I don't know who the heck he was, or where his church is. What was the name of it again? *Church of a Son of a Gun*, or somethin' or other? I sure don't remember. It's been quite a day, yes it has. Quite a day.

No way all that blood is coming outta that fancy suit. Nope. Not a chance in *H-E-double-L*. Which reminds me, the dry cleaners close at four today. Don't let me forget.

Anyhoo, like I said, it serves him right she came back and gave brother Barry a bite. He's good for nothin', and he cornholed up this funeral right good. Soon as he stops bleedin', I'ma have a little talk with him.

Dates

It's midafternoon and I'm sitting in front of the TV eating dates. One of the science and nature channels is on, but I'm not really paying attention to whatever is playing. Something about bugs.

The dates taste rotten, but this doesn't stop me from eating them. I scrape the flesh off with my teeth and swallow, then lay the slimy almond-shaped pits down in a line on the coffee table. I was told there were a hundred and forty-four dates in this bag, and that better be right, because I'm doing rows of twelve.

When I get to the bottom of the bag, I'm short by two. That bastard at the fruit store lied to me. Now my plan is ruined.

When I go to rearrange the pits into a new pattern, one of them sprouts legs. It looks like a cockroach, or some sort of beetle, but it's neither. I jerk my hand back. A second later, another one grows legs. Then a third, and a forth, and a fifth. They're on their backs, squirming and wriggling, rocking back and forth.

My DVR changes the channel, and something about the end of World War II comes on, as I race to the kitchen and open up the fridge. I grab a handful of mushrooms and run back to the room with the pit-bugs.

When I return, they've all grown legs, and most have rolled over to more mobile positions. They scatter around the room when they see me, but none of them actually cross the threshold.

I place the mushrooms, cap ends up, in the four corners of the room, then another in the center of the coffee table, where I had the pits laid out until very recently.

The power cuts out, and everything in the room flashes white. I'm blinded for a minute, but when I can see again, the mushrooms are gone, and the pits are back to being pits. I gather them up, dump them in the bag they came in, and head back out to the fruit store.

I'm going to give that bastard a piece of my mind.

Let It Out

"Just let it out, man," I tell Krem, my mullet-headed coworker, who sits beside me to the left.

"Yeah, what the fuck?" says Donald, my other coworker, who sits beside me to the right.

The three of us work together in a small, cramped room—the sort of place that's piled high with miscellany and looks like it's about to collapse in on itself. We have our backs to each other, so that we form a sort of triangle-shaped workforce, and we sit on makeshift stools, with our desks facing outward. Space is tight, which means our shoulder blades touch, and rub against each other throughout the day. I'm certain this concept was mapped out before any of us started here, in a weird plan to keep employees in seats as much as possible. Even getting up for a drink of water or a bathroom break means disrupting the other two people, and potentially causing them to keel over backwards. This, of course, affects productivity, which ultimately affects our lives outside the office. The work must be done, no matter how long it takes.

Our boss calls us his "three-pointed star", some bullshit fake praise term he probably came up with one night at the bar with his friends, thinking it would keep us motivated if he said it enough times. It doesn't. He's an idiot.

Pretty much every day Krem has these sneezing fits. They last for half an hour at least, and often longer, but he tries to suppress each occurrence, which only results in a series of stifled squelchy sounds that I have to assume cause him pain. They're probably the reason he complains of headaches as often as he does. Or maybe he just likes to complain.

"What's up with that?" I ask him. "Why don't you let your sneezes out?" It's not the first time I've asked him.

"I just don't want to. What's it to you?" Krem's a grumpy bitch, which makes him a pain in the ass to work with most days, but lots of fun to mess with when the work is slow. Sadly, that's a big part of why Donald and I have stayed at this horrible job for as long as we have. When things are slow and the boss is out, we have a lot of fun. We've played so many pranks on Krem over the years, we could probably write a book. Actually, we might.

We've switched the M and N keys on his keyboard a million times. We've shrinkwrapped his office supplies, and placed his car keys in a jar of mayonnaise. Once, we turned everything on his desk upside-down and took all the bolts out of his stool. He wasn't happy about that one.

Another time, we wrapped the desk itself in pie crust and baked it. Donald knows a guy who specializes in oversize pastry.

"I don't even know how to respond to you sometimes," I say.

And just then, Krem's face wrinkles up as he stifles a sneeze. He lets out a tiny squish-sound, then a soft *"kooooo"* as a finale, as if that would fool me.

"Don't you realize the damage you can do to yourself? There's a lot of pressure in there. You could break your brain."

"Whatever," he says, dismissing me as he wipes a tear from his eye.

Donald laughs, and shakes his head. We all go back to work. That is, Krem and I go back to work. Donald goes back to what he does best, which is origami. Any chance he gets, he's folding paper into something fairly incredible. I keep waiting for him to come up with some sort of origami-themed prank, but I haven't seen anything yet.

I like to keep an eye on Krem, even when my back is to him. My webcam is broken, so I've rigged a tiny mirror up in the corner of my monitor. That way I can see what he's up to without being too obvious. This is good for a number of reasons. I don't really trust him, and lately I've been coming home with joke stickers stuck to the backs of my shirts. Obviously this is payback for some of the pranks we've pulled. But, as far as I'm concerned, his retaliation will not stand. Miserable bastard.

Most of the time, I don't even use my computer. My job consists largely of removing garbage text and stray characters from hard copies of company paperwork. I get rid of inappropriate quotation marks, erase extraneous exclamation points, and cross out asterisks wherever I find them. Crossing out asterisks can be especially difficult, but I have a few tricks.

Today, however, is the sort of day that happens just once a month. I'm on the computer, laying out the company newsletter. Part of this task, each month, is to somehow incorporate all the characters I've deleted from all the other company documents in the prior twenty-seven to thirty days. I have to keep records of everything I get rid of, then re-type all of it, since the company destroys their digital records of everything, in favor of hard copies. Go figure.

Anyway, I'm halfway through laying out the newsletter when I hear a familiar intake-of-air sound, and my eyes immediately dart to the mirror. Krem's eyes squeeze shut, and I feel his shoulders jerk against my own. I don't hear a thing, though. I turn my head, and I'm just in time to see his right ear burst like a popcorn kernel in a microwave.

A thin trail of blood drips from the swollen pink mass, which no longer resembles an ear, but looks more like a giant speckled wad of chewed up bubblegum leaking raspberry syrup.

"What the *fuck?!*" spurts Donald, who jumps up from his stool, scattering paper everywhere. He wipes a drop of Krem's blood off the back of his own neck. Krem looses balance and lurches backward a bit, and grabs his ear. Then, with the tips of his fingers, he pulls a bit of mullet forward, assumedly to cover some of the damage.

"Come on, guys. Just leave me alone, will you? I'm not bothering anyone." He never once turns to make eye contact with either of us. Donald and I just stare at each other with gaping mouths, and expressions that could only read as shock-horror-hilarity.

"I fucking *told* you," I say, jabbing a finger in his direction with every word. "You *never* fucking listen."

He doesn't respond.

Eventually the moment settles and we go back to work. There's still a lot to get done today. Frankly, I could use some help from Donald, but he's obviously got something else in mind, and I can't wait to see what it is, so I leave him be.

Our boss swings through a moment later with his leftovers from a lunch out with clients. He stops to tell us all about each course of an epic meal none of us could possibly afford with what he pays us. He knows this. What an asshole.

Of course we all have to stop what we're doing and feign interest, pretending to be impressed. He continues his description of the lavish French meal he just enjoyed, mispronouncing the name of nearly every dish, all the while staring down at us with smug eyes. We can't wait for him to leave.

Eventually he does, exiting the room while gently massaging his gut, and seemingly never noticing the mutant ball of exploded flesh on the side of Krem's head. Or perhaps he does. He's tough to read sometimes.

An hour passes, and I've made some progress. I'm three quarters of the way through the newsletter, when I hear Krem behind me once again. He inhales two short but deep breaths, then shifts in his seat and pauses a moment before letting loose a squishy, wet *P-POP!*

"Ooooh," he whispers on a stream of exhaled breath, and I glance sideward, ready to laugh, but simultaneously afraid of what I might see. And then, there it is: a pair of translucent red splotches on his monitor, and two eyeballs dangling from their stalks, like twin pendulums keeping time on his face.

"Seriously, Krem," I say with a smirk. "I think this is becoming a problem. Don't you?" Silence.

Donald stands and spins around, so he can lean back on his desk. His shoulders rise and dip with the laughter he's trying, but failing, to suppress. I can see all his teeth.

"Just let 'em out, dude," he says. "You'll be so much happier. I promise."

I shake my head, and start laughing out loud myself.

"Oh, *come on!*" I say, with some degree of force, attempting to emphasize the ridiculousness of the situation. "I mean, do what you want about the sneezing, Krem, but, you know, maybe it's time to go see a doctor."

"No."

"What do you mean 'no'?"

"Can't. No health insurance."

"What are you talking about? We all have insurance."

Krem looks defeated. Perhaps more so now, due to his lack of proper eye placement.

"Not me," he says, spinning his head in my direction, his eyes bouncing lazily along his jawline. He tells me he can't afford it on his salary, and it quickly dawns on me that I'm probably making a lot more money than Krem, even though he's been here much longer than me, and that he realizes this too. We're all severely underpaid, but it seems that Krem's situation is borderline criminal. I sense that he's known all this for a while, and that it's probably a big part of why he's so miserable. Still, big surprise. Life's not fair.

Our boss must be on the phone with someone. We can hear his laugh booming through the walls. It's hard not to take it personally, especially now.

A few minutes later, we're all back to work again, although I'm not sure how Krem is managing to get anything done. The walls stop pulsing from the jubilance down the hall, and soon our boss rolls through the room again, on his way out the door for good. He doesn't say goodbye to anyone, but we all know he's not coming back, because he never does. If you asked him, he'd say he's always working, but I've been here for six years now, and I've never seen him put in a full day. He's told us in the past that every day is a near-constant series of client meetings, which is why he spends long periods of time outside the office. Strangely enough, though, we never seem to get any additional business from these myriad clients of which he speaks. We don't even get their names. It seems he just stops into the office for a quick phone call, or to change his shoes, or maybe a quick game of Tetris, and then he's out the door again, most likely to go do whatever he feels is worth doing.

So off he goes again, and we're able to relax a bit—at least as much as we can without backs on our chairs. We still have a couple hours left before we can taste the freshness of the outside air.

Donald spends the rest of the afternoon making origami at his desk with a big smile on his face. Every now and then he flicks a paper triangle at me, asking if I want to play football. I shake him off, though; we've had plenty of interruptions today already, and I need to get this newsletter done before I leave.

Next thing I know, he's talking softly to himself as he folds, his stupid grin never wavering. Eventually I realize he's saying "paper, paper, paper, paper, paper..." on a loop.

I turn my head as slowly as I can in his direction, trying not to arouse Krem's suspicion. I have a feeling there's another prank in the works, and I see that Donald has constructed a fairly elaborate paper funnel by somehow connecting all the triangles he's made.

"Paper, paper, paper," he continues, just a hint louder. I watch him slide his desk drawer open silently, and pull out some sort of glass container. He opens it, pours the contents into the funnel, then turns his head to make sure one of Krem's eyes hasn't rolled over in his direction.

Still trying not to ruin whatever might be unfolding, I turn back to my monitor, and try to watch the events in my mirror. Donald's broken record chant continues—"paper, paper, paper"—then changes as he gets louder, saying "pepper, pepper, pepper", and I realize what is happening. He jumps to his feet and turns, raising the funnel over Krem's head, now screaming *"pepperpepperPEPPER!"*, and lets the entire jar's worth of freshly ground black pepper fall through the bottom of his paper sculpture.

I jump up too. Krem is frozen in his seat, piles of pepper mounded on his head and shoulders, his face locked in a mid-orgasm/oh-shit-I'm-about-to-sneeze expression. Donald and I look at each other with concern, then dive in opposite directions to take cover. And then— *CHOOOOOOOOOOOOOOM!* Krem sneezes, and there's no hope of holding it in.

His entire head bursts this time, exploding outward like a time-lapse blooming flower, painting the room with speckle-splatter. For a moment it sounds like it's raining, but things quickly go quiet.

When the last drops of him have fallen, Donald and I pull ourselves up from the floor and show each other the same gaping expression. I can see the corners of Donald's mouth starting to quiver.

"See?!" he yells, pointing at the shiny red asterisk that used to be Krem's head. "We *both* fucking told you! I bet it feels better now, though, *doesn't it?"*

I get to my feet and shake my head, half horrified, half wanting to burst from laughter. The room looks like the aftermath of a lasagna fight.

"Fuck!" screams Donald. "That was *ridiculous!"* He can't wipe the smile off his face, and doesn't bother trying to wipe the blood. Krem doesn't say a word. He's obviously embarrassed. Also, he doesn't seem to have a mouth anymore.

I step back over to my desk, and go into the drawer, where I pull out a box of tissues. I toss them to Krem so he can clean up his mess, but the box just hits him in the chest & tumbles to the floor. He doesn't even move.

"Damn," I say. "And another thing. You might want to cut that stupid mullet off. It's not exactly the most professional-looking haircut in the world."

He doesn't respond to that either. Oh well. Whatever. I still have work to do.

Smoke Detector

In the darkness, a tiny red light flashed. The green one beside it stayed constant.

Somehow, Rip had never noticed the smoke detector on his ceiling before. He certainly hadn't been the one who put it there. He had always felt they were a hassle, having to change their batteries year after year. And he had never known anyone caught in a blaze. He figured the smoke from a fire was all the warning anyone needed.

The more he lay in bed, the more his eyes became accustomed to the dim light. He had wanted to be dreaming by now, but sleep never came quickly enough. He had grown jealous, years ago, of his ex-wife's talent for slipping into unconsciousness the moment her head hit the pillow.

So he lay there, counting imaginary sheep. It made no difference, though. Tired as he was, he couldn't even seem to keep his eyes closed.

Soon he was able to see just about everything in the room around him, despite the darkness. He saw the basket of laundry he kept meaning to take downstairs, and the dying baby cactus on the corner of his dresser. He saw the TV remote sitting right next to the TV, on the opposite end of the room, and realized how pointless that was. Through the open window, he saw tree leaves dancing in the cool breeze that occasionally entered the bedroom.

He saw the flashing red light on the smoke detector go solid.

Then he saw two tiny shapes crawl out from the side of the contraption.

Goddammit, he thought. *Bugs.*

It was an easy enough mistake to make. But he quickly realized they weren't bugs at all. They were bigger than that. Still quite small, but larger than silverfish or the German cockroaches he came across from time to time. Besides, he mainly found those things lurking in the bathroom or kitchen.

These had a roughly human shape, but with tiny tentacles instead of arms and legs. They caught hints of the moonlight from the window, and looked slimy, like slugs that had mated with starfish.

They slurped their way fairly quickly across the ceiling, toward the far end of the room, where the TV was.

At first, they didn't seem to notice Rip. But that changed when he sat up.

"Hey!" he shouted. "Just what do you think you're doing?"

The creatures stopped instantly, and squeaked like frightened mice. They didn't try to get away, however.

But they did continue to make noise. It reminded Rip vaguely of the *Chipmunks* record he had as a child.

They squeaked back and forth, obviously in conversation. After a quick exchange, there was a pause. One of the miniature monsters raised a tentacle, brandishing what seemed to be a tiny metallic gun, and pointed it down from the ceiling at Rip.

He stood up on his mattress as the creature squeaked a single word—what he understood to be a grand declaration: *"Deeeeestrooooooy!"*

A pink spark burst from the tip of the monster's weapon, but did no damage. The pair of creatures slurp-dashed back to the smoke detector, and crawled underneath.

Rip stepped to the foot of the bed, where he was able to stretch up and reach the smoke detector. He tore the thing from the ceiling easily, finding that there were no wires to attach it, and nothing hiding underneath. The red and green lights remained lit. He shook it with both hands, and heard a soft rattle from within. He smiled.

"Got you, *fuckers*," he whispered.

Then he hopped down to the floor, and bounded over to the window, where he tossed the smoke detector like a Frisbee.

Even in the darkness, he could see it spinning almost perfectly as it fell in an arc toward the back lawn. Then, just before it crashed into the ground, the red light began to flash again, and the smoke detector lit up from its underside, glowing a pale, foggy green. It swooped upward, taking independent flight, and rose into the night sky until it disappeared in the clouds.

Rip stood at the window for a moment, staring out at the trees, and the clouds, and the homes of his neighbors, who were all surely asleep. He shut the window with some force, and the glass shook in its frame. He made a mental note to buy a screen, then he crawled back into bed.

That night, Rip's house burned to the ground. But he never smelled smoke.

God

We found God's corpse down by the water, and decided to turn it into an amusement park.

At least, we assume it's God. I haven't had any prayers answered lately, and neither has Lilly. And He certainly looks the part. Long white hair, beard, white robe. Lightning bolt tattoos on both arms. And He's fucking huge. Like the size of a skyscraper. So, you know, either tattooed giants exist, or this is the Big Guy. And I don't believe in giants.

We were out walking in the woods, Lilly and I, exploring, when we found Him. His body was just lying there, motionless, absolutely titanic. At first we didn't even realize it was a body at all. We just saw the robe, wrapped around this massive...thing. It reminded me of when Christo wrapped the Reichstag, so we decided to check it out.

When we got close, sure enough, there He was, dead, His body half lying in the muck by the river that runs from one end of the woods to the other. He was already starting to rot, but it wasn't too advanced. Surprisingly, He didn't stink at all—which was weird if you think about it. I mean, if we're all made in His image, wouldn't that extend to our decomposition too?

The next few weeks were busy. We were lucky to find a construction crew willing to take on such a big project on short notice. But Lilly has some connections, and really, this amusement park idea has dollar signs written all over it, provided we get things going soon. We cut them in on the profits in lieu of regular payment, so I guess I'm not too surprised it worked out.

We turned God's head into a haunted house. The upper row of teeth was decorated to look like giant tombstones, and His nostrils made for perfect cave-like entrances. We figured having to push your way through an enormous nest of nose hair was a deliciously, disgustingly creepy way to start things off. And we set things up so that each nostril offered a totally different experience. Two haunted houses in one. That's what it's all about in the fun park biz. You've got to give the customer something new and different whenever you can. More bang for the buck.

Of course, we had to scoop His brains out. That was rotten work, with an endless stream of dump trucks hauling out who knows how many tons of pinkish-gray goop. And building a whole series of passageways, secret compartments and trap doors was no easy task either, especially in a round space, but I think it worked out pretty well. We hired some good guys. The exits are at His ears, and we weaved a sort of cargo net out of His sideburns, which guests can take back down to the ground if they like.

We separated His lower jaw for a swing ride. Honestly, this may have been one of the most involved processes in making the entire park. We've got His arms raised up in the air (don't worry—they're braced with steel girders) and His hands hold the hinges of the jaw. It's rigged so that His arms are constantly in motion, like He's turning a crank with both hands, and the jaw acts as the carriage for the riders. It swings back and forth, spins over itself, doing 360s, etc. Lilly describes it as being like the mutant offspring of a

Ferris wheel and a Scrambler. It's pretty incredible. A little unpredictable, but a lot of fun.

Actually, we're lucky we found God when we did. As I said, He was starting to rot, which meant His stomach was filling with all sorts of noxious gases. So that was job number one. We sealed off every potential exit point, and reinforced the stomach lining. Turns out He didn't have a belly button, so we didn't have to worry about that. Then we built a padded frame around the outside, and now His belly is a gigantic moon bounce. The kids are going to love it.

We've got something pretty special happening with His ribcage too, but I can't talk about that just yet. But people are going to flip. I guarantee it.

My favorite part of the park, though, has to be the roller coaster. We only had room in this part of the woods for one, but boy, is it a doozy. I always loved Space Mountain as a kid, loved the coaster-in-the-dark premise—and I think we may have actually one-upped it.

We sliced God open at the hips, and relocated His legs and pelvis a little further south. The lower half of His body was still in good shape, so we decided to use most of it for structural purposes, angling His legs in certain ways and coiling His entrails around them. One of them is bent upward, so we can have a big drop from the knee. And we implemented an electrical system, which sends impulses to shock the intestinal walls, causing them to contract, pushing the cars through smoothly. It's really something.

I'm so proud of it. And I'm very confident in saying we have the world's first inter-intestinal roller coaster. It's dark and squishy, and it's one hell of a ride.

Of course, there's plenty of other attractions too, and we've got a great staff in place, ready to go. We even have organ rafts to take people back and forth to the parking lot at the end of the river. We're still ironing out the contract with our food vendors, but I expect everything to be sorted out in a matter of days.

This park is really something special. Seriously. I can't wait for you to see it. I don't want to give everything away, though—at least, not before opening day. But that's right around the corner.

Just wait 'til you see what we did with His tongue.

Scheduled Meal Service

We're having lunch in the air. I chose the tuna sandwich, while the man beside me went with ham and cheese. All our side dishes were identical: carrot sticks, bag of pretzels, foil-sealed chocolate pudding cup.

Nothing to drink, though. I tried to catch our flight attendant as she floated by, but she was busy trying to wrangle her parachute at the time. Maybe I can get the attention of the other one.

We had breakfast on the plane, before the explosion.

It was nothing special. A pre-packaged plastic bowl of cereal. Piece of bread. Fruit cup. And a separate slice of melon, which I skipped. I never was a big fan of melon.

I'm not having any luck getting our drinks from the other flight attendant either. I'm guessing she can't hear me because of the clouds, and everybody screaming, and all the twisted hunks of metal creaking in the wind. But she can clearly see me waving at her. She's waving her arms and legs right back at me.

It seems we'll be having dinner on the ground. I'm kind of in the mood for pancakes.

Rough Night

I did not sleep well last night. Turned over this morning, and had shooting pains all around my left ear. I hate when that happens. Guess it got all folded up and twisted against the pillow. Really hurts.

Found my other ear underneath the pillow. I reattached it, but it's still pretty sore.

My back is stiff too. Not sure what I did, but my midsection looks like a wad of stretched-out bubble gum that was left in the sun to dry, then tied into a knot. If I was able to stand up, I'd probably be about nine feet tall. But of course I can't.

My right shoulder appears to be dislocated as well—which explains why I'm unable to reach the remote and shut off the TV. Looks like I've got a flight of steps running from my neck to my elbow.

It might not be as bad as my left leg, though. Must have gotten wrapped up in the sheets or something. It's bent the wrong way—forward, that is—and my foot is stuck, somehow tucked underneath my scrotum. It's unpleasant, to say the least, mainly because I haven't clipped my toenails in a while.

And the sheets are completely soaked. There has to be at least a gallon of blood here. At least.

Can't imagine what happened last night. I don't remember a thing—not even my dreams. But I do know this: I'm already late for work, and that's a problem.

Mummy Kitty

Mummy Kitty came home in bandages. I assume that's how she got her name. I certainly didn't give it to her.

I found her at a shelter, completely wrapped from head to tail. The only parts of her showing through were those golden glowing eyes, and her eighteen claws. That's six plus six plus six. Or nine plus nine.

She's stayed that way ever since. So I kept the name. I've tried to change her wraps, but she always runs away. I suppose that means she's comfortable. It's fine. She doesn't stink *too* badly.

My head hurts. My hat is making me itchy.

They told me Mummy Kitty was old. Already fifteen when I got her. *And that was fifteen years ago.* Most cats only live to fifteen. On average, at least. But Mummy Kitty is no average cat.

I've been into math recently. Just basic stuff, really, like addition and multiplication. I like to keep things positive. *(Get it?)*

The other night, Mummy Kitty started making strange noises. It was late, and I was fetching some aspirin from the medicine cabinet when I heard her clicking in the TV room.

The sounds were regular and repetitive. Machinelike.

Clickclickclickzzzzzrrrrr…clickclickclickzzzzzrrrrr… clickclickclickzzzzzrrrrr…

She's probably just dreaming, I thought to myself, although I had never seen her sleep. I may have even said it out loud. I went to bed, hoping my headache would be gone after a good night's sleep.

When I woke up the next morning, my head was buzzing even more painfully than before. I blamed the weather. The temperature had doubled since the day before. My hat made things even itchier.

All day long, Mummy Kitty walked in a circle. Over and over and over and over. I counted for a while, but gave up after a couple hours. Math can really tire you out sometimes. My headache wasn't helping.

When it was time for lunch, I called Mummy Kitty to come eat. I had prepared a delicious cheese tray for both of us, with bowls of wine. But Mummy Kitty didn't come.

I called for her again. I waved a piece of cheese in the air, hoping the scent would waft over to wherever she was hiding, but she didn't appear.

I searched the house. She wasn't in the TV room, or the dining room, or the bathroom, or the basement. She wasn't in the bedroom, or the other bedroom, or the other bedroom, or the other bedroom. There were some dusty paw prints in the hall, but that was it.

When I returned to the kitchen, however, there she was: faceplanted on the tile, as if she had been running and her two front legs had suddenly given out.

Perhaps she had gotten into the wine when I wasn't looking, I thought.

Mummy Kitty's bandages were loose. They looked slightly more tattered than before.

When I picked her up, I found that her eyes no longer glowed. Something was wrong.

As I cradled Mummy Kitty in my arms, her wraps began to unravel. Her front legs fell off, and *th-thunked* to the floor. They weren't the legs of an average cat. They were instead two decorative wooden spindles, like the ones you'd find beneath a handrail going up a flight of stairs.

What's wrong with Mummy Kitty?, I thought to myself. *Did the shelter know about her front legs? Is that why she's been bandaged up all these years?*

And then, to my surprise, Mummy Kitty fell apart completely. Her bandages unspooled further and fell in a heap. And suddenly, in my arms, I held her body: a metal cylinder with gears and wheels inside, a vacuum cleaner bag, two sets of broken broomsticks reconnected and hinged together, a curled tube of foam insulation, a tiny mechanical voice box, two tortilla chips, eighteen kernels of unpopped popcorn, and a pair of bright yellow marbles.

I dropped to my knees on the kitchen tile, and wept, screaming *"Why, Mummy Kitty, why?"* My head was throbbing. I heard static. Tears rolled down my cheeks, and my nose began to run. It tasted sweet.

I set her down on the floor, and counted her pieces, one by one. There were thirty, all told. One for each year she had been alive. I liked that. I piled them into two groups of fifteen, then ten groups of three, then five groups of six.

I squeezed the sides of my head to help ease the pain. I wiped sticky tears from my cheeks, and stood back up.

I removed my hat and scratched my head as I walked to the bathroom. Beneath my hat, I had some bandages of my own. I looked in the mirror, and began unwrapping them, slowly exposing more and more of my beehive head. Honey trickled down the sides, slowly. I dabbed at it with the bandages as the bees inside buzzed angrily. My head pulsed more and more intensely, until, finally, I had had enough.

It was in that moment that I decided to expand my mathematical horizons, and try subtraction. I grasped the sides of my beehive head firmly, dug my fingers in, and jerked upward. The last thing I heard was a gooey suction sound.

I dropped the beehive in the tub. I stood there for a moment. Suddenly, for the first time in a long time, I was minus one companion and minus one head. I felt better instantly.

Happyface

I'm woken by a soft barrage of clown balloons bombarding my forehead, just like any other morning. The long, narrow rubber-skinned cylinders have been serving as a sort of alarm clock for a few weeks now. I'm not sure how it all started, but I do hope it ends soon.

"Are you a week? Or still a schlep?"

These are the kinds of things Happyface says to me, all puns and disjointed sentences. He smiles through every word, no matter what the subject, and his jagged, irregular bits of teeth float inside a sloppy, drooly mouth the color of eggplant, poorly ringed with cheap red lipstick.

I groan and mumble something incoherent and as mysterious to me as it must be to him, before dragging my sandpaper tongue across my lips, in an effort to wet them. Then I muster up the energy to whisper "Yes...I'm up."

One of my eyes is half open, the other is still sealed. Even so, I'm able to determine that I slept face down, with my head at the foot of the bed. I'm not generally a restless sleeper, so I half-suspect Happyface is to blame. Perhaps a bit of pre-wake-up entertainment for the old clown?

"He's a week! A week! Awake!" he yells, high-pitched enough that the neighborhood dogs start yipping and yelping from down the street.

My vision's no good in the morning, but I can see his silhouette bouncing up and down, as if the hardwood floor had become a trampoline overnight. His cotton candy hair, pink with blue streaks, has the morning sunlight behind it, and for a second, I could swear he's jumping around because his head's on fire. But that's not the case. Too bad.

I do half a push-up, then succumb to my poor night's sleep, and crash back into the lumpy mattress, smashing and bending my nose upward into Lon Chaney *Phantom* territory. I roll onto my back, bouncing a few balloons to the floor, and wipe the crust from my eyes, so I can open both the same amount. Then I spin around, so my head is by the headboard again, and I can see the stupid clown without too much strain.

"Hmm..." says Happyface, "Are you sure? You don't look too *very berry* awake to me." He pulls a purple balloon, already inflated, from the quiver on his back, and loads it into the balloon gun he's holding. It looks like a crossbow mated with a super-soaker and a glittery rainbow. Not the most intimidating thing at first glance, but I've seen it before, and I'm definitely not in the mood for it today.

The purple balloons are the second worst kind you can get hit with. They sting on contact, unlike the others. The white ones with blue stripes are apparently the worst of all. Thankfully he's never pulled one of those on me. But we're not off to the greatest start this morning, so we'll see where things go.

"Hey! Who's your friend?" I interrupt, referring to the jester standing next to him on one leg. I've never seen him before. The balls he's juggling seem to go click-clack in mid-air, and I realize pretty quickly that they're actually a trio of tiny skulls, though I can't tell what kind.

"Why, that's Chester! *Chester the Jester!* On loan...er, *vacation*...from merry old England! Yes, *marigold in-gland.* Say hello, my friend!"

"Hello, my friend!" Chester says, in a horribly fake-sounding accent, and with each word, a piece of popcorn flies out of his mouth. The skulls come alive, each nabbing a piece in mid-air, and promptly grinding it to nothing. It's as if it was all choreographed, but Chester looks even more surprised than me. "Sorry 'bout that, sir," he says sheepishly.

I'm not sure what I've done to deserve this odd morning ritual. I don't even know where Happyface came from, or why. He just showed up one day, literally dragging me out of bed, and he's been showing up every morning since, even on weekends.

I suppose it would be one thing if I was able to be productive after the morning circus, but that never happens. This weird old clown just shows up to fuck with me, and hovers over me throughout the day. He gets quiet after noon, but he still hangs around, staring and smiling his rotten smile.

"Get up! Get out of bed! Drag a rake across your head!" he shouts, in mock-military-speak. "Better get up, *or I'll make you dead!*"

I sit up, but that's as far as I'm going for now. It dawns on me that this jerk has done some remodeling, and my walls are now painted with thick red and white vertical stripes. Knowing what I know about Happyface, I have to assume he used blood. My bedroom is now a demented circus tent.

Chester's eyes get big when he drops one of the skulls he's been juggling. It clacks against the floor and rolls under the bed. He looks sideways at Happyface to see if he's noticed, but it doesn't seem that he has, so he just sets the other two down on the floor.

When he squats down, I see that his hat isn't a typical jester's hat after all. Instead of three cloth points, it appears to be three wrinkled, gray elephant trunks hanging down around his head. And I can't tell where or how it's attached. I'm disturbed by this. He just looks nervous.

Happyface shoots the purple balloon in my direction, and it hits my shoulder like an adolescent punch. It stings like I knew it would, and it sticks there, sizzling a little before falling. I look down and see that it's burned a hole in my sleeve.

"What is your *problem?!* I'm up!"

"You're up! *Europe!* That's where Chester's from, you know." I just shake my head. "Now get happy, hippy! It's time for smiles, Miles!"

"That's not my name."

"Maybe not, but my name is Happyface, and that's what I'm here to give! Now get *happy!*" He goes on to tell me that that's his reason for being, his reason for these incessant visitations. *Clowns exist to make people happy.* His awkward behavior aside, it's all about the smile.

I ask him why he's never told me this before, but his response is a riddle I can't begin to understand. I couldn't even repeat it if I tried.

"I'm not exactly sure your methods are ideal. Or appropriate, for that matter," I tell him. "If you're trying to make someone happy, why treat them this way? Why be mean? Why torture them?"

Happyface loses his smile for a second, and his rotten shards of teeth disappear for the first time all morning. I can feel his stare deep within. My shoulder throbs as he leans in toward me.

"This is all I know," he says. Then his smile reappears, and he shoots me with two balloons, back to back. They're

both yellow, and they light up the room, glowing like kielbasa-shaped suns. They hit the corners of my mouth and stick there, like a pair of weird whiskers pressing into my face, trying to force a smile.

I see him pull another from his quiver, and my eyes widen. It's one of the bad ones, white with blue stripes.

Then there are trumpets. At least, that's my first thought. A second later, I realize it's Chester's hat, which has suddenly come to life upon his head. All three elephant trunks are waving around independently, like wild tentacles, with tiny slit-mouths tucked underneath. They announce themselves like a wriggling horn section, throwing the poor jester off balance. He dances around the room, trying to right himself, shouting *"Help! Help!"* with no trace of Britain in his accent.

And suddenly Happyface is thrown off his game. He sets the balloon gun down at the foot of the bed and turns toward Chester.

"ShutUpShutUpShutUp!" he yells, his voice more angry and borderline demonic than ever before. The elephant trunks respond defiantly, louder than they were at first, and seem to reach for him.

The walls of my room roll up like shades, exposing us to the outside. But the other houses are obscured by the plastic horses that have risen up out of the ground to surround us. They bob up and down as they circle. There's carnival music, and the air smells like sugar. I wonder what my neighbors must think.

Unfazed, Happyface takes a step toward Chester and growls.

"That's quite enough from you!" he says, as he puts his fingers into Chester's mouth, and rips out his pale white tongue. He reaches for him again, this time grabbing the jester's jaw and yanking downward, tearing it from his face with one violent swipe. The trunk-hat falls limp immediately. There's no blood, though—just a gaping black hole from his upper row of teeth to the bottom of his neck.

I hear what sounds like a hair dryer, and then it happens. Popcorn flows freely from Chester's face, his head a twisted, fleshy air-popper. The warm kernels are intensely fragrant, and in mere seconds, the floor is completely covered.

The room is filling up fast. Happyface lets out a high-pitched giggle.

"Get happy! Get happy!" he shouts above all the noise, jumping and dancing around in circles. Then he leaps toward the bed, and picks up the gun again. He takes aim, and fires at my head, but I spin off the bed, dodging the shot. The striped balloon sticks between the pillows.

He growls, and reaches for his quiver again, but it's empty.

I pull the two yellow balloons still stuck in the corners of my mouth, and use them like oversized chopsticks to pick up the striped one. Raising it, I spin around on one leg, a full 360 degrees, and whip the balloon back at the clown. It flies directly at him like a guided missile, landing right between his eyes. It sinks in, boring itself into his skull, drilling into the crazy brain that's been making my life hell for the last several weeks.

Happyface suddenly doesn't look so happy. Smoke pours out of his ears and mouth, and his eyes roll out of his skull, then under the bed. I hear the juggle-skulls squish down on them.

Finally Happyface melts away, turning into a blanket of yellow, oily goop that reminds me of melted butter. He coats the popcorn that has filled the room, and although I am hungry, I don't dare reach for any.

The carousel outside melts away too, vanishing into a puff of pink smoke, as the walls of my bedroom roll back down into place. The stripes have disappeared.

I stand still and take a deep breath, bracing myself for whatever might happen next. But nothing does. Minutes pass in absolute silence. Eventually I smile, and chuckle to myself.

"Well..." I say aloud, "I'm definitely happy now." And I head to the kitchen to make some coffee.

Multi-Crabs

Multi-Crabs! Multi-Crabs! Same price as regular crabs!

You'll get two abdomens! Eight claws! Twenty-four legs! And six eye-stalks! All you can eat! You'll never eat all of it!

Soft shell! Thin shell! Thick shell! Recently molted! Take your pick!

Would you like your Multi-Crab to be female, with extra roe? No problem! Does your preference include a copious amount of undigested algae? We've got you covered!

Multi-Crabs! Multi-Crabs! Same price as regular crabs!

We'll even boil your Multi-Crab alive, right at your table!

Try the Crab Legs and Crab Eggs Special! Now with extra pheromones!

Blue crab? King crab? Snow crab? No crab's better than a Multi-Crab!

Multi-Crabs! Multi-Crabs! Same price as regular crabs!

●

"Eureka!" Joe said aloud, standing up from his decades-old couch, his eyes glazed over from the strobing visuals of the television commercial. He licked his lips and stepped into his *Super-Ultra-Top-Secret Lobster Experimentation Room.*

"I'm going to be a millionaire," he said. "A *multi-*millionaire!"

A Field of Poppies

"Let's go for a walk," she says. "I want to see some nature."

"What's wrong with staying in? We've got trees right outside."

"Oh, come on," she says. "That's not what I mean. That's not enough."

"There's a whole back yard out there!" I say with a smirk.

She grabs the remote and turns off the TV. She gets up from her chair and stands in front of me.

"I want to see something *new*. Something I don't see every day."

I roll my eyes. I don't want to disappoint her, but it's been a long week, and I'm tired. I just want to sit on the couch and watch a movie, maybe doze off for a bit.

But she insists.

"I want to see mountains," she says. "I want to see water."

"How 'bout a nap instead?" I really don't feel like driving that far out of the city.

"I want to walk in a field of flowers," she says. "A field of *poppies.*"

She comes closer and grabs my wrist. She tugs, playfully, but with some force, pulling me up from the couch. Despite my words, I don't resist.

Next thing I know, there's a flash of red.

I wake up in the car, hands tied behind me, a blindfold over my eyes. My head's killing me, the base of my skull is sore and throbbing.

"Hey babe," she says. "See? You got a nap in after all."

She used one of her knockout bugs on me at home. No surprise. She breeds them in the basement, and doesn't think I know. It's not the first time she's done this. It's kind of like her way of pulling rank, so to speak.

I make a sound, but it's not even a word. I feel my heart thumping in my chest, nervous about where we're going.

"We're almost there," she says.

I feel the car turn down a smaller road than the main one we were just on, and we travel on a while longer.

"Wait 'til you see this place," she says.

Another ten minutes or so go by. I have no idea where we are, or how long I was out. She cracks the windows and I can tell the air smells different. Could be hours away from home for all I know.

I fight against the ropes binding my wrists, but there's not much point. She's a knot expert, thanks to her dad, the ropemaker.

I feel the car slow down, then stop. She gets out, and lets me out of my side. She keeps the blindfold on me, and guides me. We're in the woods—I can tell that much. I can feel the foliage brush against my legs as we walk.

"Almost there," she says. She's smiling. I can hear it in her voice. I just hope wherever she brought me is worth the bruise on the back of my neck. "Okay, stop."

She undoes my hands, freeing me up to remove the blindfold myself. It takes a second for my vision to adjust to the light, but I can see we're standing near a clearing in the middle of the woods. There's a pocket of light just ahead, where there aren't any trees. Just flowers.

"Let's go," she says, jogging ahead of me. I squint, my vision still blurry.

"Are those...*poppies?*" I ask, finally able to form words again.

"Come on," she yells back. I see her bound into the field, bouncing with pure joy. I follow her in.

The flowers—the poppies—don't look quite how I expect. They're red and white and pink and all sorts of peachy colors. Some are chocolate and olive and caramel tones. Their stems are thick, each one the same color as its flower.

They are hands and arms, legs and feet, growing straight out of the earth, sprouting among the green grass. Some of the flowers are clenched fists. Others have blossomed into open hands.

"Well?" she calls to me. "Isn't this *amazing?*"

I'm not sure what to think. I don't really have a response.

Fingers and toes wave in the breeze. I can't quite believe it.

"What is this place?" I ask. "Hey, wait up!"

I run after her, doing my best to jog through the poppies without stepping on any of them.

But I don't get very far.

The poppies grab me. They wrap their hands around my ankles, my calves. They grab my pant legs, and hold me still. In the process, I lose sight of her.

I struggle to get free, but the poppies' grip is far too strong. Even the smaller baby arms growing out of the ground are surprisingly powerful. They clamp my feet to the ground.

I hear a pop behind me. It's a wet sort of sound. I turn my head and she's standing there right behind me, smiling, gazing at me. My heart is racing.

"I wanted to bring you here today, because it seems like such a special place," she says, as she walks around to face me. She's holding something in front of her. She seems to have gotten something on her dress.

"I picked this one for you," she says.

She hands me the flower. The poppy. The arm, with its bloody roots dangling limply from the elbow. The middle and ring fingers are curled in, but the others stick out straight.

"See how this one is?" she asks. "It means...it means '*I love you*.'"

My eyes dart back and forth between her eyes and the poppy she's holding out for me.

She drops down to one knee.

I don't know what to do. I don't know what this is. My head is throbbing. And my heart... *My heart is about to explode.*

Tap, Clip, Glue

I tap my nails to make them grow. So I can cut them. So they'll grow some more.

It's the same biological concept as what happens when you get your hair cut. Your body thinks it's being attacked or damaged in some way, so it reacts with a burst. When hair gets cut, your body grows more. When there's too much friction on a spot of skin, your body makes a callous. When your nails get clipped, your body makes them grow some more.

Tapping your fingers yields a similar result. Impulses from your fingertips tell your brain that they're being hurt, so it's time to make the nails grow more.

Your body wants to protect itself, no matter how much you may want to destroy it.

But we need to destroy it, don't we? Just a little bit? We do this so we can function in this society we've made. We want to be able to see what's in front of our faces. We want to be able to use our hands. So we cut our hair and clip our nails.

I've got my own reasons, though. Domestic issues.

Not relationship troubles. Nothing like that. I'm talking home issues. Like monsters in the pipes.

This house isn't all that big, actually, but it's full of bathrooms. The guy who built the place was an architect with irritable bowel syndrome, so every room has a toilet.

Anyway, he's dead, and the house is mine now, and I've come to find that there are toilet monsters living in the pipes. This is why I clip my nails.

Let me explain.

Every day I slaughter an animal. Cows, goats, the occasional buffalo. It's not very nice, I know, but really it's just a matter of necessity, and I like to think each animal gives its life for a higher purpose. Like troops giving up life for country.

I use the larger organs—mainly the lungs and stomachs—to build my fish. Of course, I attach one of the animal's eyes, and I can usually find something to use for fins, but what's a fish without scales? That's where the fingernail clippings come in. I tap my fingertips, I clip my nails, and I glue them to the stomachs and lungs. Then I tap some more, because each fish needs to be covered from end to end, and that takes more clippings than you'd think. Tap, clip, glue. Tap, clip, glue.

I have another process I use to bring the fish to life, but it's kind of a secret. I can promise you I get no sexual satisfaction from it, however. It's purely a means to an end.

Once the fish are alive and wriggling, I send them into the pipes. I can do this from any room in the house. Then I tap my nails some more. Tap, clip, glue.

I've built a small army this way, and I think it's safe to say I've been making progress in my war with the toilet monsters. I just have to keep going a little while longer, and hopefully some day soon I can claim victory and go back to a normal life. But until then, it's tap, clip, glue, tap, clip, glue.

And if, for some reason, this war becomes completely unwinnable, I suppose I can always make a cocoon from my

hair, and change myself into something else entirely. If I can't
have a normal life, maybe a different life is good enough.

The Eater

The Eater ate. And ate. And ate.

He ate for sustenance. He ate for fun. He ate to stave off boredom. To pass the time.

He got good at it. Better than most. Soon, he began to eat competitively, and he won every contest he entered.

People were impressed. The ones in charge of the competitions even helped him get sponsorship. Soon his sponsors were paying for his bills and his fun, and for everything else.

That gave the Eater more time to eat. And the more he ate, the more refined his skills became. In time, he developed unforeseen techniques for eating things, and a variety of new chewing patterns. He honed muscles no one else had ever used, or even heard of.

He was able to eat faster every day, and swallow with more power than ever before. He turned eating into an art form.

Soon, he began to eat things no one else had ever successfully digested. Pheasant fuzz cakes, mango knots, snowflake biscuits, dog webs, muck melon, brain stripe sausage.

He became famous. He appeared on television regularly, where journalists and celebrity chefs would take turns interviewing him. He was offered roles in movies, and large amounts of cash by rich men attempting to get him to sleep with their daughters.

People hand-delivered gravel pies and home-made ostrich cakes to his public appearances. They shipped fluffmuffins and tire pops to his fan club headquarters. And he ate them all.

Time passed, and the Eater wondered if there was any end in sight. Would his fans always be there, cheering him on? Or would his fame gradually begin to fade away? Was there really that much more he could contribute to the world of eating? His agent said yes-yes-yes, but he still wasn't sure.

Eventually, after many, many months of pondering where this road would take him, the Eater started having some new thoughts. Dark thoughts. Among other things, he began wondering what it would be like to eat some of his fans.

This wasn't something he really wanted to do. It was more of a compulsion. Something he felt he had to do—or, at least, something he might not be able to stop himself from doing. It was something his body seemed to want.

He tried to suppress the idea, to bury it deep inside, beneath so many layers of mashed flipsteak. But it wasn't easy. He tried to keep busy instead—to keep his mind occupied—spending the hours eating anything and everything else. He filled his days with dither toast, goblin loaf, fruit flags, and grilled nurblies. But it didn't matter much.

The dark thoughts hovered in the background, ever-present. When they surfaced from time to time and he found himself unable to block them out, the Eater began to gnaw on his own knuckles.

He continued eating other things. He wondered if it was possible to eat so much that he would grow sick of eating altogether. Or could he simply stop on his own?

What do you do when the thing you love—the thing you're best at—becomes a living nightmare?

One day, while chewing on the side of his finger, the Eater broke through the skin. And he realized the problem might be even more serious than he thought. He realized in that moment that he had a taste for blood. Salty, savory human blood. He ate three trays of raw skunkwiches instead, hoping that would satiate his desire.

That night, like every other night, he returned home, belly full, to his extravagantly unusual home, which was known as Head House. He stood on the street outside for several minutes, breathing deeply. Who could help him? Who could he reach out to? He hadn't spoken to his agent in weeks, and his sponsors were just corporate entities who seemed to deliver messages only when he wasn't available.

The Eater's stomach gurgled, reminding him that his body was in control of what it wanted, and his mind had no say in the matter.

He removed his shoes on the street, and strolled barefoot up the spongey, pink walkway. When he reached the entrance to Head House, a pair of soft, pink oversized lips parted just enough to allow him in, before resealing themselves around him. Then Head House swallowed him down to his subterranean bedroom.

That night, the Eater slept in the cozy warmth of his home, terrified, hoping that when the sun rose, and the eyes to Head House opened, that he would not be regurgitated back into the day.

Otto

Even after the process was complete and people could finally see the end result, they still didn't get it. But then, Otto had always been misunderstood.

Was he just hoping to become a better swimmer? If that was the case, friends told him, there were classes he could take. Swimming lessons could be arranged anywhere from a private gym to the community pool. Before things got to the point of no turning back, some even offered to pay for them.

Was it his love of mutated comic book villains? Surely there were better things in life to emulate. Had he not learned the lessons contained in some of those books? Those who were considered unique, or different, were often punished, or exiled, or forced to live life in the shadows. Was he planning a life of crime? His friends and family never would have expected such a turn of events, and certainly couldn't condone it.

Otto's coworkers seemed convinced he just wanted to become a better multi-tasker. He was unquestionably a go-getter in his work life, but this still seemed a bit extreme for most. Even so, a few coworkers found the process intriguing, to say the least, and while they may not have thought it was a quote-unquote normal thing to do, they would raise their eyebrows, purse their lips, shrug their shoulders, and say "Sure, I get it. Wouldn't do it myself, but I can see why someone might."

But it wasn't about multi-tasking, or swimming, or comic book villainy.

When Otto was discharged from the hospital, he took a few days to recover. He informed his job that he wouldn't be returning at all—not unless there were unforeseen complications with his surgery down the road.

And then, on a Monday morning, Otto stepped outside his apartment and walked down to the corner, where he spent the rest of the day, and every day after.

A placard hung from his shoulders. The back panel explained what he had done, and why. He shared his reasons, which boiled down to his belief that the world was running out of love, and that he needed to step things up, and share as much as possible with as many people as possible.

It also explained how he had raised the money for his operation online, and how he had located two surgeons willing to do what he wanted. One had removed his perfectly-functioning arms, and the other had replaced them with a pair of live octopi.

The front panel of Otto's placard read, simply, *"FREE HUGS"*.

Landau Made Some Mistakes

The first mistake Landau made was choosing a helmet made entirely of tuna salad.

If he had bothered to spend any time whatsoever thinking his decisions through, he would have realized what a bad idea that was. Tuna, of course, had never been used structurally in outer space before. Surely he could have guessed that the mayonnaise would break apart in zero gravity. But he had been more focused on getting the ship built and into the air.

Landau would come to realize his error in judgement soon enough, however. Moments into his first spacewalk, his helmet, already weakened by the atmosphere, was devoured by hungry space-cats. They rushed at him from the void of space, at all angles, mewing between the stars, purring furiously as they attacked the tuna with their elongated space-cat bodies and their extra-coarse sandpaper tongues. Mere seconds later, the astronaut found himself without protective cover.

Whoever said you couldn't hear screams in space was full of shit.

Of course, the sound of Landau's screams only sent the space-cats into a deeper frenzy. Once the tuna helmet was gone, they licked his face furiously, while simultaneously clawing at his suit. His cheeks turned red quickly, suffering abrasions from the animals' tongues. Thankfully, however, the claws of these particular space-cats were dull, so his suit suffered relatively few tears.

The astronaut encountered a stroke of good fortune when a small cloud of space dust and debris floated past. The detritus confused the cats like a drug, and he was able to break free from their flailing fur-lined limbs. He pulled at the lifeline attaching him to the side of his ship, and managed to tow his way back quickly, long before the space-cats regained their composure.

Landau was met at the ship's hatch by Donna, his pilot. They had met through an ad he placed online, looking for space-companionship, just a month before blasting off from his back yard.

She struggled with the door for a moment, but eventually popped it open, and hoisted Landau back into the ship by the back of his collar.

"You okay?" she asked. "I must have forgotten to warn you about the cats."

"I'm fine," Landau responded, huffing. "Did you know you can actually breathe out there?"

"Err...*really?* I don't recall anything about that in the space guidebook."

"Well, sure enough, it's no problem. I was kinda freaking out when those things ate my helmet, thinking I was about to suffocate in the deep darkness of space, but yeah, I just kinda took a breath and realized the air's just like it is at home. Pretty weird, huh?"

"I'd say so," Donna replied, wearing an expression of concern. "Let's get you out of that suit. Are you hungry?"

"Yeah, sure. Maybe a sandwich?"

A few hours later, Landau was reclining on one of the couches in the ship's cockpit, watching the stars through the front window, which used to be the windshield of a Dodge Caravan. Donna was at the controls, guiding the homemade ship's path through the glittery darkness.

For a small ship, there was plenty of room for two people. Landau had installed two hide-a-bed couches in addition to the pilot's chair, a relatively spacious closet, a kitchenette, and a fold-down table that could be used for playing board games. There was a stationary bicycle too, which helped with both exercise and generating power when needed.

At the back of the cockpit was the mushroom wall. Landau didn't care much for mushrooms, but a few days prior to blast-off, Donna had asked him to install it. The mushrooms seemed to thrive in space. They were practically all Donna ate.

Watching a distant comet streak across the sky, Landau sighed audibly. He was happy to be safe and relaxed, and happy he had met Donna before embarking on this adventure. With her driving the ship, he was able to sit back and enjoy the view—which, after all, was the point of the entire excursion. He had always craved travel.

"How do you feel now?" Donna asked.

"Just dandy. Although my belly's starting to rumble again. Might be time for dinner. Or breakfast. Whichever. I've completely lost track of time out here. Didn't even think to bring a clock." Landau stood up from the couch abruptly. "Wait, *what the heck is that?*"

"I don't see anything..." replied Donna.

"Are you serious? *Look!*"

"Hmm... Oh, that?"

"Yeah, that cloud up ahead!" Landau exclaimed. *"Be careful!"*

"Nothing to worry about, my friend. That's just a big space-cat hairball. They're everywhere out here. I've been dodging them left and right the last few hours. I'm surprised you didn't notice before."

"Oh jeez. Well, now I feel dumb."

"Don't worry about it. Here, grab the wheel for a minute and I'll go get you something to snack on before lunch."

Donna returned to the cockpit a few minutes later with some crackers, but dropped them to the floor in the sudden turbulence that had overtaken the ship. The entire structure shook wildly, as wires sprang loose from overhead, and pieces of metal paneling fell from the walls. Landau was standing, his hands on the wheel, trying to wrangle control of the ship. Donna raced toward him.

"I...I...don't know how to..." he said, struggling with his words as much as the ship's steering mechanism.

"What's the problem?" Donna asked, annoyed. She grabbed the wheel from Landau and steadied the ship within seconds. "Didn't you build this thing?"

"Yeah, I just...I'm sorry."

"I've got it. Go have a seat. Those cracker-shards on the floor are for you."

Landau grabbed a small metal panel that had fallen to the floor, and collected the broken crackers onto it like a plate. He sat back down and crunched on the snack bits while Donna corrected their course.

"Guess I should've just put the thing on autopilot, huh?" she said.

"Yeah, I suppose. Sorry about that." Landau chewed the last of the cracker pieces into a paste and swallowed. "Oh, sorry. I guess I should've offered some of these to you."

"It's okay. They're not exactly my favorite anyway."

"You know, Donna, I sure am glad you answered my ad. I don't know what I'd do without you. Who knows if I ever would have even gotten this thing off the ground."

"Oh, I'm glad we met too," Donna replied. "After all, without this ship, I might never have found a way back home." She stood up from the controls, placing the ship on autopilot, and turned to face Landau.

"Huh? Back...*back home?*"

"That's right. You know, it's a shame you managed to get away from my friends out there. You were meant to be a sort of travel souvenir from me to them. Like salt water taffy after a trip to the beach. Or a much more delicious snow globe."

Donna licked her lips and nose, and shot a sinister look at Landau. A chill traced his spine, as he suddenly realized that his second mistake had been trusting her.

"You've probably noticed I haven't eaten much on this trip," Donna continued. "Well, that's because our diets are...a bit different. I do love those mushrooms, but they just haven't been quite enough. I've grown hungry these last few days, you know."

As the words escaped Donna's lips, her human face—a facade—began to crack and break away. The same happened with her spacesuit and the human-like flesh beneath it. A long, fluffy tail rose up behind her, as her slender tongue reappeared and wiped the remains of her shell away, revealing her true elongated-feline form to Landau.

"*Space-cat!*" Landau gasped.

"And now it's time for me to feed!" she announced, mewing loudly, before darting at her prey.

Landau jumped up immediately, and leaped over the back of the couch. It wasn't much of a barrier, however. Donna pounced right over it, clawing at him in mid-air.

Landau winced at the pain and scrambled out of the way, falling toward the other side of the room, landing on his back side. At the same time, Donna smashed into the wall, then landed softly on all fours.

The astronaut's eyes darted all around the cockpit, searching for some kind of weapon, but he foolishly hadn't planned for any adverse conditions that might require the use of force. He had stocked the fridge, brought plenty of blankets, and installed numerous redundancies for powering the ship, but hasn't thought to bring anything with which to defend himself, should the need arise.

He spider-walked backwards across the room as Donna arched her back, wagging her furry tail violently from side to side. Landau reached the mushroom wall, pulled a few caps from it, and tossed them to the floor in front of Donna. They made no difference.

"It's over, astronaut. Just let this happen," she said, purring. She stared him down, waiting for him to make the next move. When he didn't, she pounced.

Landau dashed sideways to avoid the claws headed for his face. Donna missed him, and crashed into the mushroom wall.

Meanwhile, Landau scrambled back toward the couch. He spotted a piece of scrap metal—his cracker plate—and snatched back up in his hand, slicing a fingertip on the ragged edge in the process.

Donna spun around and prepared to pounce again. But before she could make her move, Landau hurled the piece of metal in her direction. His shot was perfect, connecting with the side of Donna's neck, slicing through the fur and flesh, revealing her bright pink insides. Landau kept his eyes wide open as the cockpit was showered with a torrent of crimson.

Donna the space-cat dropped to the floor in a heap, splashing into a puddle of her own blood, which expanded rapidly across the cockpit floor.

Landau collapsed too, in relief, and sat for a moment to catch his breath. He stood, trying to remember if he had packed a mop, and glanced out the front window.

Directly ahead was a massive hairball, at least ten times the size of the one he had seen earlier. Before his eyes, it stretched outward, like a net, being pulled at the edges by dozens, if not hundreds, of angry-looking, hungry-looking space-cats. They had built a trap, and he was headed straight for it.

Landau snapped up his space guidebook in a panic, realizing that his third mistake was not learning how to pilot his own damn spaceship.

The Smile

I made the purchase online, and two days later, a box appeared at my doorstep. It was brown cardboard, wrapped in brown paper, tied shut with a single length of yellow string. My name and address were printed on the outside, as were the following words:

Contents: 1 Smile

I scooped the package up and took it inside, hoping none of my neighbors had noticed. I did not open it immediately, however. I wanted to wait, and I was faint with hunger.

I made dinner, but did not enjoy it.

Later, after having digested my meal, I sat quietly in my library, staring at the package, which I had set down on a small table. For some reason, I resisted opening the box for several hours, though I was unsure why. After all, I had placed the order. Surely I wanted what was inside.

It wasn't until midnight that I made the decision.

I retrieved a pair of scissors from a drawer, and clipped the string surrounding the box. I sliced the side of the outer wrap, and peeled away the brown paper. The cardboard box within was sealed with tape, which I also used the scissors to cut through.

I sat with the box a moment longer, before opening the corrugated flaps.

The smile, no longer constricted by cardboard, floated softly upward, out of the box, and hovered in front of my face.

I felt relief then, and a sense of happiness I had been, prior to that moment, unable to articulate. I stared lovingly at the smile, barely noticing as the lips parted, just slightly, to expose a pair of gleaming, pointed fangs.

The smile flew toward me, diving for my neck. I was too slow to dodge it. The smile opened wide and sank its fangs into me. It stayed planted on the wound, sucking, drinking, draining me.

Finally, when the smile sensed how weak I had become, it pulled back, and hovered again in front of me. Then it dove in again, and attached itself to my face, replacing my own mouth.

I'm happier now. The smile is in control. It keeps me up all night, and makes me sleep through the day. It makes me venture out into the darkness, to sneak upon the unsuspecting, and drain them of their essence.

The moment they turn from who they were into this horrible, beautiful new thing, fresh smiles form on their faces. It is as if they appear from out of the ether, replacing their own sad mouths.

And I am compelled to steal their smiles, to peel them from their faces with numb fingers, leaving the rest of their bodies to rot in the grass.

I take their smiles home and place them gently into small cardboard boxes, which I later seal with tape, then wrap in brown paper, then tie closed with string, before sending them out into the world, to the saddest people I can find online.

The Magician

Footlights illuminated the stage of the small theater, their output bleeding onto the foremost ripples of the red velvet curtain hanging down from the rafters, sectioning off the performance area from the space behind, where, in theory, the real magic happened.

Left of center, the curtain itself began to wriggle and jerk—softly at first, then rather violently—until, suddenly, the magician found a break in the fabric, and emerged.

He was dressed in a formal tuxedo with tails. He wore a black top hat. His gloves, vest, and bow tie all matched the pristine white of his dress shirt.

The magician approached the front of the stage, and smiled at the crowd assembled before him. He removed his hat, and placed it, top down, upon a small wooden table that had quite magically appeared through a trap door in the stage without anyone noticing.

The magician displayed his gloved hands for the audience. They held nothing. He moved his hands in the air, keeping them constantly visible. He interlocked his thumbs and flapped his fingers, pantomiming the motions of a bird in flight. Then, in the blink of an eye, a living, breathing bird appeared. A dove. He held the bird up for all in the audience to see, and it flicked its wings, shedding a piece of a feather, which fell softly to the stage below.

With a flourish, the magician waved his other hand in the air, and brought it down beside the bird. Several members of the audience gasped as a second dove appeared alongside the first. The magician now had one bird in each of his palms. He spread his arms apart, then brought his hands back together, and raised them up directly in front of his face.

The birds attacked suddenly, lunging at the magician's face, pecking out his eyes almost as instantly as they had come into being. Blood squirted out, and streams of it rolled down the magician's face, dribbling down onto his shirt, as the tattered remains of his eye stalks fell to rest on his cheeks. But he made no sound at all. The audience applauded.

Without the benefit of sight, the magician managed to feel around for the wooden table beside him, and placed the two red-beaked doves down upon it.

He reached a hand into his jacket pocket, but brought it out empty. He reached into the opposite pocket, but his search yielded the same result. He seemed to stare deep into the crowd with his empty eye sockets, crimson trails glistening beneath them.

He raised a finger to the audience, his glove now speckled red, as if to say "Just a moment! I have an idea!" Then he reached to the table to retrieve his top hat. The doves startled, but did not attempt to fly away.

The magician held the hat aloft for the crowd to see. He tipped it forward to show that it was empty inside, then back to display the solid quality of its top.

Then, with one hand, the magician held the hat near chest-level, as he reached inside with the other. He seemed to reach further in than was physically possible, his arm disappearing up to the elbow. He seemed to feel around the vast inside of the hat, unable at first to find what he was searching for. Then, the hat itself began to shudder and wrench. The magician struggled, one hand inside, the other beneath, until the sound of a loud crunch resonated and echoed through the hall. The magician froze.

Extracting his arm from the hat, the magician revealed his hand, and a portion of his arm, to suddenly be missing. Instead, he held up the ragged, bloody stump that remained, surrounded, barely, by the wet, tattered edges of his sleeve. Blood spat from the place where his arm now terminated, spurting in crimson arcs to the floor, forming a small puddle. The audience gasped.

The magician dropped the hat to the stage and stomped on it. Without the use of his eyes, he initially missed several times, but eventually landed the blows he intended, causing the hat to crumple and flatten under the weight of his foot, before kicking it with his heel to the red curtain behind him.

The magician turned his focus back to the audience, and took several wobbly steps forward. The wet stump at the end of his arm glistened in the footlights. The magician stumbled, and nearly fell over. Then he stopped, and once again raised his hand—the one still attached to him—and extended a finger.

This time, he reached inside his jacket, and into the small side pocket of his blood-stained vest. From within, he retrieved the corner of a white handkerchief, still perfectly clean. He pulled the cloth to his stump and dabbed the wound, absorbing some of the blood. Then the magician raised the handkerchief to his head, to wipe away the red tears streaming from the pair of holes in his face.

The handkerchief, now removed from the vest pocket, had a secret of its own, however. At its opposite corner was a knot. The white cloth was connected to another, this one blue.

The magician let go of the white handkerchief and pulled at the knotted corner of the blue one, only to reveal that the blue piece of cloth was connected to a yellow one. The magician kept pulling. The yellow handkerchief was knotted to a green handkerchief, and the green handkerchief was tied to a pink handkerchief. The magician pulled and pulled, and soon the stage floor was piled high with cloths of every color imaginable.

And then the magician hit a snag. The handkerchiefs stopped, as if the last one was somehow attached to the inside of the pocket. The magician would not be deterred, however. He pulled harder. He tugged and tugged at the last piece of cloth until it gave way. And finally it did.

At the end of the last handkerchief was a knot. And on the other side of that knot was a piece of pink rope.

The magician continued to pull. He pulled meters and meters of soft pink rope from his pocket, unable to see his intestines slowly coiling atop the pile of handkerchiefs on the floor at his feet.

The lower half of the magician's vest turned red quickly, just as his knees gave out. He held his hand and stump out for the audience once again, as if to show there was no trickery afoot.

Then, the magician collapsed. The audience cheered.

Flesh is Flesh

Flesh is flesh...is flesh. Beef or chicken or pork—it makes no difference to me. They all taste pretty much the same after the first few bites.

Same holds true for the more exotic meats—antelope, rattlesnake, black bear. You know what they say: *"Tastes like chicken!"* And it's true. But most of the time chicken tastes like nothing.

How about dog? Or cat? Or rat? Sure, you say it sounds disgusting, but is it really? Do you know for a fact that any of these would taste worse than a sloppy, mud-painted pig?

What about us? Hmm? What about *human* meat? Guess what, people—Flesh is flesh. And we taste like chicken.

I watched a chicken eat a dog once. And a rat eat a cat. There's a pig in my kitchen right now, staring at me, with mean eyes and a cleaver pinched between his hooves. There's a cow in here too, wearing an apron and a chef's hat. She looks ridiculous, but she's great with a knife.

It's cramped inside this oven. Probably should've had the bigger one installed. I asked the chicken on the rack above what she thinks we should do.

"Bok-bok! Bok!" she said, and I know what she means. Flesh is flesh...is flesh.

Blow-Up

Bob Flanksteak: Independence Day festivities have been marred by tragedy, as area man Karl Bloom unexpectedly blew up in the University Heights section of the city this evening. Witnesses say they were struck with pieces of what could only be described as...*Karl Bloom,* while trying to enjoy an evening with family and friends. Channel One's Claudia Trufflebottom spoke with area residents about this terrible tragedy.

Claudia Trufflebottom: Bob, I spoke with area residents about this terrible tragedy, and these are some of the things they said...

Agnes Flurp: Yeah, I knew him. Well, part of him, anyway. Flew right past my kitchen window. I was making enchiladas.

Marcus Haystack: Y'ask me, and I'll tell you. It was the drugs. That needle they stick in their arms is like a bicycle pump. Not literally, of course, but metaphorically, yes. Now, I don't know what kinda crazy explody-drugs are out on the streets these days, but this is a big problem in our community, and I won't stand for it.

James Variable: Karl blew up? Like, *exploded?* Shit. I didn't know. I heard somebody say he blew up...I thought he just put on some weight. Or got pregnant or something. Wait, *what?*

Josie Puppydog: He had too much soda. That's all. Plain and simple. Too much soda. Too many bubbles. There's a reason they call it soda pop, you know. Drink too much, it makes you go *pop!* You should see my two-year-old. He blew up twice last week.

Malcolm Goodenough: Spontaneous combust-a-plosion. Right? That's a thing, right? I'd check with the government on that. Oh, and lasers. You've seen Real Genius, right? Government's shooting people with lasers from outer space now. Space lasers. That's why I carry an umbrella with me at all times. No way that's gonna happen to me.

Ellen Squeezercheeks: He was a sinner. That's what God does to sinners. He blows 'em up. Oh, I'm sorry—did I say sinner? No, no—he was a swimmer. God does not like swimmers.

Chad Standup: I—I just don't believe it. Karl was great, a real dynamite guy. No way this really happened. There's just—Hmm? You have pictures?

Nadine Null: Well, one thing I can tell you about Karl Bloom is he sure liked his jigsaw puzzles. Heck, I wouldn't be surprised if he did this to himself, just to see if he could put himself back together.

Steven Firmshaft: No, no. I know the truth. Seedy as it may be, I know what caused that poor boy to explode. But it isn't pretty. It isn't family-friendly. The newspapers probably won't even report it. But I'll tell you. See, Karl was a bit of a...*pervert,* pardon my French. He had a thing for those blow-up sex dolls. Had a collection of them, from what I heard. *Dozens.* Well, if you knew Karl, you knew he was a hefty fella. Not tiny. No sir. He was a big'un. Well, he was surely doin' his business one night, if you know what I mean, playing hide the salami with one o' them dolls. Well, he must've put too much weight on the top half of that old inflatable lady, and all that air just shot straight up his pecker. And *BOOM.* Good for her. He was a sick one, that Karl. Y'oughta give that doll an award.

Claudia Trufflebottom: Well, Bob, as you can see, the opinions of Mr. Bloom's former neighbors have some wildly different opinions on the man some are saying enjoyed sexual relations with inanimate objects. One thing they can all agree on now, though, is that Karl Bloom definitely exploded tonight, and now lies dead all over University Heights.

Bob Flanksteak: Thanks, Claudia. And rest in pieces, Karl Bloom. And...oh, it appears we have some breaking news... Multiple sources, including one Chief Investigator, are now reporting to Channel One News that Karl Bloom, in fact, willfully ingested four sticks of dynamite before leaving his home this evening. It seems he ate dynamite, and subsequently blew up. So...there you have it. I guess that's it. End of story. Thanks for wasting our time with a bunch of crackpot theories from various area lowlifes, Claudia. Now here's Jack Highspeedchase with Sports.

Melt

He takes a sip of the solution, then snaps the capsule in front of his face, releasing a tiny puff of gas. He inhales it.

It doesn't take long.

His eyebrows begin to droop. His cheeks sag. His eyelids fall slack.

The skin on his forehead drips downward softly, like ice cream melting in the sun. It covers his eyes.

His ears detach too, each one dipping cockeyed away from where they're supposed to be. They somersault in slow-motion, flipping themselves over onto his neck.

The cartilage of his nose cracks softly, and the skin around his nostrils drips and melts into itself, sealing off the passage of air.

His lips drop, and soon dangle well below his chin. It becomes difficult, though not impossible, to breathe.

A tiny sigh of relief escapes.

He doesn't have to watch the news. He doesn't have to listen to his neighbors fight any longer. He doesn't have to smell the garbage in the streets. He can't see the cockroaches in his kitchen, or the bills he gets in the mail, or the woman from down the street with the black eye that seems to change sides from week to week.

He lives in his own head now. He still dreams—and sometimes those dreams are nightmares—but they're temporary. They're not real. They fade away with the morning light. Not that he can see it anymore.

So he never hears a thing about the Pennsylvania zombie uprising. Or the giant silkworm attack in Beijing. He can't see the thousands of people in riot gear right outside his window. He can't hear the helicopters, or the explosions. He doesn't smell the smoke creeping through the building as the flames engulf it.

And he is happy. He's never been happier.

666 Baby Jesuses, Give or Take

The thing about Baby Jesuses is, they're everywhere. In a way, I suppose that's kind of the idea, but what I mean is, they're not all in one spot. They're not clustered together like a bunch of grapes, or a group of inmates in a prison. They're more like Easter eggs, all spread out and tucked away in hidden places. Which, again, is probably how it's supposed to be. But my point is, this makes collecting them rather difficult.

I found my first Baby Jesus under the couch, enrobed in a fine coat of dust. It was purple, with slightly darker-purple polka dots, and I nearly tossed it in the trash, before I realized what I had. I brushed the dust off, and he giggled, ticklish. Then he coughed up a tiny knot of phlegm, which was just about the cutest thing I had ever seen. And that's when this little addiction of mine began.

I found the next one baked into a loaf of artisanal bread, which I picked up from the bakery down the road. The bread was a rosemary-olive focaccia. The Baby Jesus was lemon-flavored, with poppy seeds.

The third Baby Jesus had leopard spots. The fourth was decorated with the Italian flag and a tiny mustache. The fifth had raisins. The sixth was covered with old sailor tattoos. The seventh had cat ears, whiskers, and a long tail that waved lazily from side to side. The eighth smelled like cinnamon.

Soon I was finding a new Baby Jesus almost everywhere I went, whether I was looking or not. There was one in a hanging folder in my filing cabinet at work. Another was clogging one of the gutters at my home. I nearly stabbed the one hiding in my Pad Thai with a chopstick.

Before long, I had collected a hundred of these little guys, each one unique in its own special way, each one tucked away in some strange corner of my day-to-day life. Some were alive, and behaved themselves, like cute, cuddly, smiling cherubs. Others were like tiny statues, leaving me to wonder if they were the preserved corpses of dead Baby Jesuses, or just fabrications in the image of the original Baby Jesus. If there was, in fact, an original. If there was, I wonder what it looked like—what color, what flavor, what scent.

Some of my first hundred smelled like vinyl and paint, while others reeked like garbage. Most were fine, though, and smelled soft and fresh and clean, just like any other baby.

They're mostly the same size, these Baby Jesuses, like little teacup kittens. I can hold pretty much any one of them in a single hand if I'm careful about it. And I have been. I haven't dropped one yet.

A few are larger, though. Like the one I found when I cracked open an egg for breakfast one morning. That one seemed to grow slowly, like a sponge in water, until it was the size of a small suitcase. A small, moist suitcase. That one stays in the sink.

I found a bunch of tiny Baby Jesuses on the tops of my ceiling fan blades. These guys are pretty small, actually— like little Lego men. They'd fit nicely into a dollhouse if I had one, but since I don't, I was thinking about building something. Probably with Legos.

I decided to use some of them as accessories. Most days I've got one of these guys pinned to my lapel, but of course I have to change it out every day—to go with whatever I'm wearing, but also to keep things fair. I don't want any of them getting jealous.

Once I hit two hundred Baby Jesuses, I knew I really had something. A real collection. Something that took work. Something to be admired.

I bought pedestals and display cases for some of my favorites, playpens and baskets for others. Most of them now live on the shelves of my bookcases, though. I had a yard sale to make the space, and whatever didn't sell went straight to a used bookstore downtown.

I found my two hundred and fiftieth Baby Jesus on the side of the road, lying motionless, dressed as a hobo clown, tire treads all down his left side. Poor thing.

Number 251 was carved out of wood. He's stained beautifully too, but has a pair of plastic googly eyes stuck on, which I think is a little tacky.

Number 264 was a mini, found in a box of chocolate-covered peanuts I bought at the movies. I cleaned him up in the movie theater bathroom while a worker mopped something off the floor of one of the stalls.

Number 312 has a long neck, like a giraffe. No spots, though.

Once I had four hundred Baby Jesuses, I started going to church on Sundays. I had never been a particularly religious man, but four hundred Baby Jesuses have a way of changing a person's mind about things.

At the coffee hour after the service, I asked around, but no one else had a Baby Jesus collection, which I found surprising. Nobody I talked to had even a single one. Most people said they hadn't even been looking.

I'd found the majority of mine without looking, though, so it all seemed a little suspect to me. *Were these other people hiding their collections away? Was I taking part in some competition I didn't know about, where everyone was keeping their Baby Jesus number a secret, so as not to let anyone else know their standing in the game? That might be.*

Or was I just special? Could I really be the only one in town with a Baby Jesus collection?

The next day I decided to kick my collecting into overdrive. I called in sick to work, and started hunting.

I checked every corner of my house that I hadn't checked before. I found one stuck to the inside of a lampshade, and another in a box of cereal. There was even one hiding inside the sleeve of my original *In-A-Gadda-Da-Vida* album. I can't find the record, though. I'm starting to think maybe he ate it.

I found a few more out in the yard. There was one dressed like a ninja hiding in the bushes, and another with a red bandana around his neck, balanced on top of the fence.

My next door neighbor wasn't home, so I decided to check his house. I knew his back door had been giving him problems lately. It wasn't tough to jiggle it open. Good thing he didn't have an alarm.

Anyway...*jackpot.* My neighbor had a pretty impressive collection himself, but probably never realized it. They were everywhere—under chairs, in closets, floating in the toilet tank—and they were some of the most unusual ones I've found.

One of them was covered with dozens of eyeballs, which all seemed to leak little bloody tears. Another was wrapped with gold foil and smelled of chocolate. One seemed to be made of compressed dryer lint. Yet another was, I assume, made of soap. It seemed to foam up whenever I touched it, tiny bubbles effervescing all over its surface.

Once I had gone through the entire house, I gathered all my new Baby Jesuses up in a laundry basket and took them back over to my own house.

The next logical step, of course, was to visit the homes of my church congregation. I fixed a quick snack, then went back out on the hunt.

Sure enough, each of my fellow church-goers had plenty of Baby Jesuses hiding in and around their homes, though I still don't know if they knew it or not. They could have just as easily been unaware as they could have been trying to hide their collections from everyone else. Tough to say.

In any event, I'm happy to report that none of these people were home, and that breaking into their houses was extremely easy.

I got a Baby Jesus with a Viking horn helmet, and one dressed like a cheerleader with fluffy pom-poms instead of hands. I got one that looked like a little Bonsai tree. There was one that glowed in the dark, and another that was brown and furry, and had four arms and four legs, and basically looked like a Baby Jesus spider.

One had a hook on its back, like a Christmas tree ornament. Another seemed to be made of peanuts and caramel. And still another one had camera lenses for eyes and a red button on its side.

The last house on my list belonged to an old lady named Gladys. She was actually home, but that turned out to be a good thing, because I found a little red Baby Jesus inside her chest, tucked behind the ribcage, nestled against her heart.

And there was another one inside her dog, but I'm not sure I want to get into what I had to do to retrieve it.

I took everything home in a shopping cart I found on the side of the road. Once I got back, I did a quick count and realized I had about 665 Baby Jesuses now. At least, I think so. I got a little mixed up in the middle of the count, and didn't feel like starting over.

Anyway, with 665, I figured one more should do it, since 6 was my lucky number.

I took a break. Sitting down at the kitchen table with some coffee, I remembered reading something years ago about how Jesus probably didn't look like the blonde-haired, blue-eyed image we're all so used to seeing. Given the part of the world he was supposedly born in, he probably had dark skin.

I took a gulp of coffee, and nearly choked. I recovered quickly enough, though, and spit a little Baby Jesus back into the mug. He was dark brown, almost black, and looked like an oversized coffee bean with little arms and legs. He even had that coffee bean split running down his back. Super cute.

So of course I took this to mean that my collection was pretty much complete. It was an obvious sign. I had 666 Baby Jesuses, give or take, and that was good enough for me.

I pulled my best suit out of the closet—the one I'd been wearing to church all these Sundays—and got the safety pins out.

Luckily it was a good, solid suit, made of quality material. I had inherited it from my grandfather, but never wanted to wear it until recently. And now, it was about to become the greatest, most important suit in the history of ever.

I pinned my entire Baby Jesus collection to it. Every single one of them. It wasn't easy, mind you, but I made it work. I put the mini ones on the vest, so they wouldn't bulk things out too much. I needed to be able to fit the jacket on over it. The bigger ones went on the back of the jacket, which had the most real estate.

When I was done, the suit was a thing of beauty. It took some time to put it all on, but once I was wearing it, a sense of accomplishment washed over me. It's actually a little tough to describe how I felt, wearing that suit. There was something special about it. All I can really say is, it was the greatest feeling I had ever experienced. And it was the most comfortable suit I had ever worn, even though I couldn't put my arms down to my sides.

I left my keys and wallet on the kitchen table, as I wouldn't be needing them any more, and I stepped out the front door of my house, not even bothering to pull it shut behind me. From the porch, I looked up to the clouds, squinted at the sun, and pulled in a deep breath.

I exhaled, and everything felt perfect. I was ready to face whatever, or whoever, might be waiting for me along my path. Not that it mattered. I had my suit on.

Then I started moving, one Baby Jesus-cloaked step after another. I walked to the church, knowing that I had more Baby Jesuses than anyone else—and a suit to pin them on—ready to step through those doors and declare myself the winner.

Story Notes

The Regenerates:
Written in a house in the woods, on a mountain. The floor of the bedroom my wife and I were staying in had mysteriously soggy carpeting, which I assume somehow led to the creation of this story. That doesn't make much sense, but then again, maybe the story doesn't either.

Violins For Sale:
So far, this is the longest short story I've ever written (cue the sounds of most of my writer-friends laughing uncontrollably). It's also one of my favorites. This originally had a very different second half, featuring a pirate with a rude surname battling Dr. Damage in the street. I like this version much better, but the pirate may still show up somewhere someday.

Wrecking Ball:
Occasionally I'll be struck with a very simple image, and I just start typing to see where it leads. When I write this way, the stories tend to be very short, but they're a hell of a lot of fun to write. The film referred to here is *The Tenant*, and the song that samples lines of dialogue from it is "The Choke" by Skinny Puppy.

Playtime:
Some people get very serious, and sometimes downright mean, when they're really just supposed to be having fun.

Cat Tree Summer:
I've written a number of stories that feature cats, which strikes me as funny, because I'm allergic to cats and generally can't be around them if I want to be able to breathe and use my eyes. And I generally like to breathe and use my eyes. This story came to me during a long weekend getaway in the Poconos. It was written mostly in one sitting, in a lounge chair by the water, to the sounds of egrets and hawks flying above.

Sweets:
As a child, I never found clowns to be particularly scary. As an adult, I'm terrified of the people who make them.

Hole:
A stream-of-consciousness story sparked by a small wound on my chest.

Drive:
I remember seeing an interview with Nivek Ogre of Skinny Puppy (yes, them again) mentioning something about scientific experiments on chimps, and somehow, this came out.

Horns Up:
I spent a good portion of my teens and twenties at metal concerts, although I never really looked the part. My tastes eventually took a turn for the more electronic and experimental, but I still go to metal shows from time to time. Hopefully what happens in this story never happens to me.

We Built the Moon:
Some people think the moon landing was faked. Others think the moon itself is fake.

The Bigot:
A quick Frankenstein-esque revenge tale for the bleeding-heart liberal in all of us.

The Pet:
My stories feature animals quite frequently, you may have noticed. This is one of them. Or is it?

Slices of Me:
This collection originally had a different title, and the stories were in somewhat of a different order. Then, as I was polishing everything up and getting it ready to send out, inspiration struck, and I wrote this late one night and early the next morning. It was an uncomfortable writing experience—so I knew I had to add it to the collection and change everything around.

Brother Barry:
Originally written for a zombie anthology called *Rotting Tales*. The prompt for every story in the book was a piece of artwork, which would eventually become the cover art.

Dates:
This is the first story I wrote that I really considered to be "bizarro". I had written other things in the past that would probably qualify, but in my mind at least, this marked some sort of turning point in my writing. My friend, artist Amze Emmons, drew a minicomic adaptation of this, and we had a bunch of them printed a few years back. I still have a few, which I sometimes sell at conventions or give away as prizes.

Let It Out:

Over the years, I've gotten an obscene amount of creative inspiration from coworkers. More of this story is true than you might think.

Smoke Detector:

Inspired by old sci-fi movies, the *Twilight Zone* episode "The Invaders", and the little light above the bed that winks at me when I'm trying to fall asleep.

God:

I gave a reading of this story once, in a dirt-floor basement with crude wooden benches and strings of Christmas tree lights illuminating the space. I think two people came to the event, and they both left before I got up to read. I wonder if they would have enjoyed this story or been offended by it.

Scheduled Meal Service:

I wrote this a few days before getting on a plane, and of course it was on my mind the entire flight. I didn't mention anything about it to my wife until we got back home. I am a considerate husband.

Rough Night:

Just a description of how I usually feel in the morning.

Mummy Kitty:

Substitutions spring up in my stories frequently. I used to focus on this a lot in my artwork, assembling all sorts of found objects into replicas of other objects. My old apartment used to look like a warehouse full of spare parts. For everything.

Happyface:

Written with the intention to submit to an anthology of weird clown stories. Either I missed the deadline, or the anthology was cancelled—I don't remember which—but either way, I never sent it anywhere else. Happyface is excited to finally have a place to call home.

Multi-Crabs:

I used to want to work in advertising. I love coming up with ridiculous commercial ideas for ridiculous products. I'm not sure I'd enjoy coming up with commercials for real products now, though.

A Field of Poppies:

I have a thing for body horror, and body parts. This is also very apparent in my first book, *SuperGhost*. I can't explain why. Perhaps another decade or two of writing stories like this will eventually reveal the reason for this obsession.

Tap, Clip, Glue:

Probably inspired, at least in part, by the trauma of being a homeowner.

The Eater:

This thing knocked around in the back of my head for years, and it took more changes and adjustments than I ever could have imagined for a story of its length. I've probably revised this story more than everything else I've ever written, combined. I'll probably want to make more changes as soon as this is published.

Otto:

Nice people are weird, huh? They really tend to stand out in our culture these days.

Landau Made Some Mistakes:

Inspired by a postcard advertising a local artist's gallery show. Unfortunately I don't remember the artist's name, but the image featured an astronaut whose head and helmet were entirely covered by cats. I took this story, untitled at the time, along with me to my first BizarroCon in 2013, and got some great feedback during a workshop run by John Skipp, and filled with a bunch of bizarro writers I greatly admire.

The Smile:

A very recent story, and the first vampire thing I've written in many, many years. I have no idea what prompted it, but it came to me, and I wrote it, in a dark room around midnight.

The Magician:

Story ideas can come at any time, so it's good to take notes before they evaporate. I keep a file on my phone, which I add something to, even if it's only a title or an image, almost daily. Often, something comes to me as I'm waking up in the morning or falling asleep at night, and ends up haunting me for days. That was the case with this. By the time I sat down to write it, the entire thing had congealed. There's something about this story I find deeply unsettling. It plays in my head like a short film that came into being completely on its own, without the aid of a director or actors.

Flesh is Flesh:

Another early bizarro piece, which was written for a contest. The idea, as I remember it, was to take a line or title from one of author Michael Arnzen's stories, and run with it. So that's what I did. Weeks later, I got a postcard from Mike thanking me for the story, and offering some nice writerly encouragement.

Blow-Up:

An early bizarro piece that I can't really explain, and barely remember writing.

Melt:

Another very recent piece. I read this to my wife upon completing it, and it bummed her out.

666 Baby Jesuses, Give or Take:

Inspired, in part, by Bearbricks, the small plastic figures made by Japanese company MediCom. Similar to Lego minifigs, Bearbricks come in the form of a simplified, cuddly, potbellied bear, which various artists and designers create their own patterns and designs to apply to. There are thousands of different designs in existence. This is starting to sound like a commercial. I better stop.

About the Author

*Scott Cole is a writer, artist, and
graphic designer living in Philadelphia.*

*He likes old radio dramas, old horror comics,
weird movies, cold weather, coffee, and a few other things too.*

Find him on social media, or at 13visions.com.

Printed in the USA
CPSIA information can be obtained
at www.ICGtesting.com
LVHW092155051024
793032LV00014B/124